MAGNETIC ANOMALY

A Seaman's Yarn of the North Atlantic Ocean.

Richard Woodman

First published in 2021 by Sharpe Books.

For Arlo, with love.

CONTENTS

Author's Note	i
One	1
Two	28
Three	51
Four	70
Five	108
Six	124

AUTHOR'S NOTE

As with most 'action' fiction, at some stage the author asks his or her reader to suspend their disbelief, an implicit process to which the reader, if he or she persists in learning the outcome of the story, agrees. However, I am not indifferent to the degree to which any reader might ask to what extent my yarn is based on fact, for *Magnetic Anomaly* has its roots in personal experience.

The narrative is set in the winter of 1966 and while the *Weather Guardian* is entirely my own invention the ship depicted here is – or should be – a mirror image of a reality. Almost all the detail is culled from a journal I kept at the time of my service in a British Ocean Weather Ship, though the narrator is, of course, an imaginary figure. Moreover, his narrative reflects contemporary attitudes, including the long held tradition that ships were invariably referred to as 'she'.

Likewise, Captain Gordon and his ship's company are fictional, though Second Officer Pennington owes his inspiration to the star-crossed careers of two men, only one of whom actually served in a weather ship. There, however, the resemblance ends. Pennington's character, his personal details and his odd belief-system are completely fictional, though it has to be said that among the seafarers of my time were to be found many men whose 'take' on the human condition was no less extraordinary than Charles Pennington's. These could vary from followers of the Buddha to enthusiasts for the precepts of Prince Piotr Kropotkin, with grades of opinion – political and spiritual – of all types.

One rather amusing and true source was an old Quartermaster who had seen service in the Royal Navy during and after the Second World War. This stalwart claimed to be the only sane man on the ship we were both then in, because he alone had a certificate to prove his mental state!

Although equipped and intended for ocean rescue (chiefly of air-liners in those early days of trans-Atlantic air-travel), I never participated in an event such as is related herein, mounted from an Ocean Weather Ship. However, I subsequently did so, on a number of occasions, from an entirely different class of vessel, and in a number of different capacities. As to the matter of handling a ship's boat in heavy weather, this too I have had the opportunity to experience in all its exhilarating terror on an almost routine basis (such was the nature of my employment at the time).

There are, apart from the matter of the old Quartermaster's sanity, three true events which directly link me to this tale of a weather ship in the North Atlantic. The first is the fact that one night on my watch a Dutch air-liner did report engine trouble and reversed her course; the second is that a vessel *did* put out a call for assistance which she later cancelled and the third was that utterly daft wintry overnight drive to Greenock. This was something of a marathon in those days, particularly in an open-topped and elderly sports-tourer.

This tale of the sea is the fifth – and I hope the final – novella I shall have written during the Covid-19 pandemic of 2020/2021, produced against a back-ground of tragedy not unmixed with Brexit. As I remarked at the beginning of this note, it was born out of shreds of personal experience and the lives of others during a long period when people of my age have had ample time to reflect upon the extent and experience of their lives. If it should find favour with any readers, I should like it to be seen as an homage to the men who, half a century ago, manned these odd little ships and who were – for my money anyway – a tribute to the British Union.

Readers interested in Ocean Weather Ships will find an excellent and informative web-site at www.oceanweatherships.

Richard Woodman.
March 2021.

1

I suppose it started as a modest adventure of my concoction in that mad-cap car-ride from London to Greenock, back in December 1966. I hated the long, exhausting over-night train journey from Euston to Glasgow Central. If one couldn't afford a sleeper, and I certainly couldn't, there were little in the way of comforts to be obtained. I seem to recall a tea trolley on the platform at Crewe, and a hurried descent from the train to buy a paper cup of sweet orange beverage, along with a curled sandwich, but that was about all. If you were lucky enough to have fallen asleep, you could miss this benison, but that was unlikely because all too often the British Rail heating was poor. And if the chill did not keep you awake, your fellow passengers probably did, for we departed from Euston not long after closing-time and many of one's travelling companions brought a carry-out with them. And since many of these were squaddies from one or other of the Scottish Regiments on their way home for a spot of leave, released at last from the constraints of Army discipline and with their tails well up, the companionship was boisterous, to say the least.

Often it was down-right dangerous, for these young men had all-too-often returned from foreign postings where they had lived under very real stress and partaken of acts of violence that today would have constituted trauma, and invited counselling.

So the civilian *Sassenach* sitting in the corner was an open invitation to some degree of ribbing which, if his responses were considered by the pack to be offensive, all too easily degenerated into a verbal assault which only ended with the soldiers falling asleep. I did try and travel with another member of the ship's company once, but that only seemed to invite twice as much piss-taking and general unpleasantness, so I came up with the idea of joining ship another way: I would drive and take a passenger who would help with the cost of fuel.

Although most of the ship's crew were Clyde-siders, or Scotsmen of one sort or another, a smattering of us came from England, especially the heads of the scientific departments and the younger specialists who had yet to settle-down, marry Scottish girls and live near the Ocean Weather Ship Base at Greenock, on the lower Clyde, west of Glasgow.

During my previous tours of duty I had made friends with Ted Wilkins, the Assistant Meteorological Officer, who lived in Surrey with his parents. Ted was a year older than me, and my senior in rank, having – when we were at sea – two gold bars under the royal crown on his shoulder boards. As Third Officer I only rated one, but we had first joined the ship on the same day, and struck up an immediate friendship. He was a career meteorologist and had been serving at a land station for some while, so he did not have any experience of ship-board life, whereas I had been at sea for six years, having begun my career at sixteen, trading out to the Far East in fast cargo-liners. In all that time I had only risen from a cadet to Third Mate so, with, promotional prospects poor, and rumours of redundancies consequent upon a company merger, I had decided upon a change. Besides these factors, I had met an attractive young woman named Sukie with whom I had thought I should spend the rest of my life. Long trips of four or five months were, I knew, inimical to a happy marriage in those hippy days, so I had cast about for something that, at least for a while, gave me a stepping stone ashore or to some more congenial, maritime-based employment.

The Ocean Weather Service seemed to offer such a half-way house and would certainly do for a start. Exceptionally generous leave almost amounting to month and month about was a major attraction. Less of a lure was the pitiful pay, but I was young, I did not intend to make the Service my career and I thought a few trips in the North Atlantic would widen my experience. I was not be proved wrong.

So it was that I arranged with Ted that on the expiry of our next leave, I would pick him and his gear up at Edgware Station, one end of the Northern Line, at six o'clock on that winter evening. Accordingly, having got my twenty-year old MG TC Tourer out of its lock-up near the house of my widowed mother a few miles away, shoved my own kit behind the red leather bench seat, checked the engine-oil and filled up with petrol, I rolled into the forecourt of the tube terminus with about three minutes to spare.

Ted gave the car the once-over. I had bored him with accounts of it – British racing green, red radiator grille and brake-drums, twin SU carburettors and so forth, all greatly beloved attributes of a young man's personal vehicular transport in those days. But I don't think he had actually realised that along with all this, the owner had a penchant for driving with the hood down!

In actual fact, even though it was December, with a rug round one's knees, the engine heat kept the passenger quite warm and for me, the driver, the sense of freedom and of *travelling* was a potent drug.

Anyway, we jammed his gear in behind his seat, he tucked himself in and off we went. Not much in the way of fast motorways in those days; Edgware lay on the old Roman Road of Watling Street, the A5, which headed north. Our little adventure had begun.

We stopped a couple of times to drink hot coffee from a large vacuum flask, relieve ourselves and wolf-down some sandwiches, thundering along at a respectable sixty plus miles an hour under a cloud of frigidly silver stars until, thirteen hours later, with a watery sun rising through a low bank of cloud to the eastwards, we drove over the snow dusted hills of Clydebank into Greenock and pulled up alongside the ship as she lay, double-banked, outboard of a sister Ocean Weather Ship, in the 'Great Harbour'.

Stiff as a pair of hatch-boards, we humped our personal effects through the slush and up the gangway, across the deck of the inner vessel and aboard our own. Having dumped our bags in our cabins Ted and I drank a large mug of hot, sweet, tannin-laced tea made from the hot-water boiler in the wardroom pantry. The ship was not in full commission, she was cold, inhospitable, miserable even, and had only a skeleton crew on board, so we were obliged to go ashore in search of a breakfast. After scoffing a huge platter of bacon, eggs, sausages and fried potatoes, washed down with more hot sweet tea in the local 'Greasy Spoon,' Ted returned to the ship. I left the MG with a garage that offered cheap storage facilities for officers with cars in the Ocean Weather Service, and walked back to the ship where I turned in, absolutely knackered.

When I woke and emerged from my cabin about mid-afternoon there were decided signs of life. My cabin radiator was warm, not warm enough, but the fact that steam was seeping through the ship was welcome. Whilst I had been in the Land of Nod, others had been joining the ship and the cabins along the port alleyway – set below the upper, forecastle, deck – were filling up. I could hear doors banging, greetings being exchanged, mostly in Scots dialect and mostly consisting of that mild and fraternal abuse used by men exchanging one world for another, marking the transition from land – and usually wife and bairns – to our rugged place of work, the steel tub that would be our home for the next month, out on the broad and inhospitable bosom of the Western Ocean.

I was still fuzzy with my long and arduous drive so, having donned my uniform blue battle-dress, I made my way back to the wardroom in search of more hot tea and perhaps a friendly face besides Ted's. There were only two people in the wardroom, Dougal Henty the Second Engineer, and Iain Mackenzie, the First Officer, sitting on the settee along the ship's side. I exchanged greetings, asked if they had had a good leave and was told a fresh pot of tea and some biscuits were available in the pantry. The cooks and stewards had begun embarking stores, but there would be a High Tea of a sort at six o'clock, with proper routines starting at breakfast the following morning.

'We're due to sail tomorrow, on the high water aboot fourteen hunder. Will ye ha'e a look at all the fire-extinguishers and check the lifeboats before noon tomorrow, Jamie,' Mackenzie said amiably as I sat down stirring my large mug. His words were uttered as a question but given as an order.

I nodded. 'Of course Iain,' I responded; we were pretty laid-back as regards titles and rank, especially in the wardroom.

'Did ye drive up after all? I haird you were thinking o' it.' Dougal Henty asked pleasantly.

'Yes,' I replied with a grin.

'You must be mad,' Henty responded, turning to Mackenzie, 'they're all mad these Englishmen.'

I knew he was joshing me and I laughed. 'It was a great drive,' I said, 'under the stars, over Shap…'

'Ower Shap, eh, Iain?' Henty said, ribbing me relentlessly. 'And under the stars too! I didna ken what Ah was missing tucked-up in the lee o' Bum Island…'

'Och the lad'll learn,' Mackenzie remarked, smiling back at me, then adding, 'we've a change of orders, Jamie, we're bound for Ocean Station INDIA instead of JULIETT.'

'So no skinny-dippin' fur ye, ye mad bastard,' Henty said.

Ocean Station JULIETT, spelt with two 'T's for some reason, was west of the Shannon estuary in Ireland and a lot further south than INDIA, which lay on the same latitude as Cape Wrath, the north-west corner of Scotland. As for INDIA's longitude, it was 019º 30' West, the meridian running south through the middle of Iceland. Four voyages earlier, just before I had joined the OWS *Weather Guardian*, she had been assigned to JULIETT. The late summer weather had proved warm and the sea so inviting that half the ship's company had been swimming. Such events which broke the rigid routine of an operational Weather Ship – of which more later – became something of a wonder. It was significant that Henty still felt in warranted mention.

'You'll get nae sich fun on INDIA at this time o' the year,' remarked Mackenzie.

'Aye, we'll likely have an o'er shitty Christmas,' added Henty lugubriously.

'You forget,' I said, 'I've already done two trips to INDIA…'

'Weel bless ma soul, Iain, did ye ken the lad's done *two* trips to INDIA?'

'Oh, bugger off,' I retorted without rancour. One got used to such jibes, there was no malice in them, but they did remind me that – six years at sea or not – I was still a newcomer to the Ocean Weather Service, and a *Sassenach* to boot.

I finished my tea and was about to leave them when Mackenzie said, in respect of the ship's Second Officer: 'Och by the way, Davie Erskine's taking a voyage off. He's we bit poorly…' For a moment my hopes rose as I envisaged promotion to acting rank, but they were as swiftly dashed. 'The Third Officer from the *Weather Follower*'s coming aboard as Acting Second Mate. He's senior to yourself, Jamie, sae nae promotion fur you, Ah'm afraid.'

'Story of my life,' I said, shrugging.

'He'll nae be aboard until tomorrow mornin',' added Mackenzie, 'had to cut his leave short.'

'What's his name?' I asked.

'Charles Pennington…'

'Och it's oor Charlie is it?' put in Henty, hearing the news, like me, for the first time.

'Aye. It is,' responded Mackenzie to his side-kick, 'he o' the uterine passage!'

Pennington's name meant nothing to me. Moreover, being a junior officer in the company of my seniors, I wrote off Mackenzie's peculiar mention of 'the uterine passage' to some obscene in-joke between the two of them regarding Pennington. Furthermore, I took no immediate notice in that brief exchange between the First Officer and the Second Engineer of anything other than the fact that the ship's regular Second Mate was ill and his place was being taken by someone else, someone who was my senior in the Service. I *was* a bit miffed, of course; I should have liked to have shown what I was capable of in the superior rank but I already knew that as Third Officer I bore as heavy a responsibility during my watch as either the Second or the First. It was our ancillary duties that were different. Anyway that was the way of the world.

I rose from my seat. It was already dark and through the wardroom ports I could see the bright-burning deck lights of the Athel tanker discharging molasses on the far side of the dock.

'I might as well take a look at the internal fire extinguishers before tea,' I said, by way of excusing myself.

*

There's a sequence at the beginning of the film *The Cruel Sea* where the tyrannical First Lieutenant of the Flower-class corvette *Compass Rose*, played by Stanley Baker, attempts to get one over on his two junior Sub-Lieutenants by asking them peremptorily 'how many fire extinguishers are there on board?' One of the two neophytes, both of who have just joined their first warship from civvie street, is terrified by the man and flummoxed by the question. The other, played by Donald Sinden, comes up with a number, fourteen I think it was, which satisfies his superior and mystifies his fellow Subbie. 'How did you know that?' Sub-Lieutenant Ferraby asks Sub-Lieutenant Lockhart. 'I didn't,' explains Lockhart, 'I was guessing he didn't either,' or words to that effect.

I was always reminded of these two young men, the one callow, the other sharp, whenever I walked round the *Weather Guardian* on my inspection of the ship's safety equipment – especially her extinguishers. The ship was not a Flower-class corvette, though the first batch of four British Ocean Weather Ships that had entered service in 1947 to provide weather forecasting data and air-sea rescue facilities in mid-Atlantic had all been former Flowers. The *Weather Guardian* and her three sisters were a later and slightly larger class of anti-submarine corvette, the Castle-class. OWS *Weather Guardian* had begun life as HMS *Weobley Castle*, named after a small fortification on the northern shore of the Gower Peninsula in South Wales. Predictably her naval nickname had been 'Wobbly Castle' and I had already learned that, notwithstanding her change of name and purpose, she was decidedly wobbly and rolled and pitched abominably. It was a considerable change from the fast cargo-liners which I had grown accustomed to.

*

The meal that evening – a sort of high tea – was adequate but unimpressive. I had not seen much of Ted Wilkins during the day. He too had had a kip, after which he had been mustering the considerable amount of meteorological stores that had to be brought aboard from the Base by his team of Assistants. The wardroom was only partially full; there would be late arrivals that evening, with the local men not joining ship until the following morning when I had to muster them all on the ship's articles. After tea a number of the gathered officers decided on a run ashore, but I had neither the money nor the inclination for the dives of glorious Greenock, being somewhat hung-over from my lack of sleep, so I turned-in early.

I woke about 06.15 to a ship gathering herself for her sea-duty. My cabin radiator was now hot, there was a short queue for the officers' showers and a mug of tea on my bunk-shelf when I emerged from my ablutions. Breakfast was a scene of coming and going, largely eaten in silence or low conversation and I was out on deck in time for an informal making of colours in which the duty able-seaman sauntered aft and hauled our defaced blue ensign up to the gaff on our tall main-mast where it joined an array of aerials, sensors and other gismos. The *Weather Guardian* was, by this signal event, back in commission.

By 09.00 I had completed my inspection of the fire extinguishers and by the time morning coffee could be smelt I had all but finished checking the lifeboat stores. Since no-one had touched anything since the end of the last voyage, these jobs were swiftly accomplished and after coffee I took a walk along the quay to take a photograph of the ship, working my way round to the other side of the dock in the cold wind to where, close under the stern of the much larger Athel tanker, I was able to get a good view of her.

The aesthetic qualities of ships are very subjective, usually confined to comments on such arcana as 'the fine sweep of her sheer,' 'the sharp rake of her bow,' or the 'elegance of her stern'. But no amount of squinting one's eye, or turning one's head slightly on one side, could induce even the most partial enthusiast to find anything of beauty in the OWS *Weather*

Guardian.

She had been conceived in wartime, designed in wartime and built in wartime. If her utilitarian bulk had anything to commend it was a simplicity that argued she had been constructed among her siblings by the mile and cut off by the fathom. It was true that, despite what seamen euphemistically call 'her lively motion' - by which they meant her inherent desire to move under their feet to a tiresome degree, rolling, pitching, corkscrewing, scending and – in really heavy seas, falling off into any deep wave-trough that she encountered, she was a remarkably fine little sea-boat. Having been built as a hunter and killer of U-boats, she had a large spade rudder and could turn on a six-penny piece.

Moreover, although many ships do possess something that makes their overall design rather fine on the eye of a discerning mariner, this is never the case with a conversion. The *Weather Guardian* was, at heart, a redundant corvette, a poor enough man-of-war in the first place, low down on the scale of British naval majesty. Although her 'Atlantic-grey' hull remained very obviously that of a small warship with a long forecastle and a short and lower afterdeck – no more a maindeck than a quarterdeck - upon the bright light-orange structures of her upper-works conversion had wrought something resembling a collection of garden sheds.

Starting at the forward end of her forecastle, with its brace of anchors and merchantman's windlass, her raised circular gun-platform now bore a steel cube instead of an open-breeched 4-inch gun. This contained a sophisticated winch the drum of which was wound round with a very, very long length of fabulously expensive steel wire. 'Piano wire,' we irreverently called it, on account of its thinness but its tensile strength was impressive. It was used for taking deep-sea soundings, of which more later.

Abaft the former gun-platform rose in two steps the main bridge housing accommodating the senior officers' cabins, the Communications or Radio Office, with its rows of radio transmitters and receivers, and the Radar Control Office. The fore part of this upper-work was topped with an anti-submarine Squid mortar, which occupied a small deck all of its own. This was moth-balled, but maintained as a potential weapon should the Cold War turn Hot. The upper level of the forward superstructure bore the navigating bridge: a central wheel-house, behind which lay the chart-room, and a walk-round deck on three sides. Above this, the highest deck on the ship, rose an ugly lattice mast in which was concealed a crow's nest lookout and a massive tracking radar array. This complex construction, what most would call a scanner, was directed from the Radar Control Office below. In purely naval terms it was an obsolescent air-search device, long superseded in front line service, but perfectly capable of following our radio-sonde fitted balloons that were launched every six hours, regular and precise as clock-work in all weathers and all sea states.

So much for the main bridge housing. Immediately abaft this the funnel revealed the presence of the boiler rooms deep in the ship's hull. The *Weather Guardian* boasted two unpressurised Scotch-boilers, though for reasons of economy we were not allowed to flash-up a second boiler unless steaming to an emergency location. This confined our top speed in moderate seas to about 10 knots. This was perfectly adequate for our routine duties, the only time when we were making anything like a passage being going to, or coming off our oceanic station. Aft of the funnel was the engine-room skylight, below which our traditional power-plant of a triple-expansion steam reciprocating engine was Dougal Henty's particular pride and joy. Flanking funnel and skylight on either side of the ship rose a pair of Welin- Maclachlan davits, in the curves of each of which nestled our two motor lifeboats, No. 1 to starboard and No. 2 to port.

Further along the deck rose another steel box, this time no more than seven feet. This was chiefly taken up by the ship's galley, thoughtfully placed on the exposed upper deck so that the oil-fired stove would not endanger the ship if it caught fire for any reason and ensuring that it was rare to receive one's grub piping hot in the wardroom, the petty officers' or the ratings' messes in the body of the hull below. This crude aedifice was entered through a pair of donkey-doors and its denizens, two cooks and a galley-boy, catering for a ship's company of just under sixty men, wore sea-boots most of the time, for the Atlantic was apt to sweep through their place of labour whenever it had a mind to.

Yet another structure arched across the ship just abaft the galley. On each side was a stores and lifesaving gear locker and from the deck above rose the main-mast with its several antennae, sensors – including two anemometers - and the ensign gaff already described. The main-mast was flanked on each side by a 40mm Bofors gun, kept moth-balled for the same reason as the Squid mortar further forward.

Thereafter came the break of the forecastle and a long deck-house containing the Meteorological Office which, like the other specialist centres, including the chart-room, was stuffed with the instruments and facilities each department needed to fulfil its function. It is probably worth noting here that the Met. Boys considered themselves the ship's boffins and intellectually superior to the rest of us. To emphasise their devotion to their black art, on the outer door to their secret sanctum, renewed every voyage just prior to our departure with a fresh specimen, hung a large piece of sea-weed. According to old seafaring lore, the bladder-wrack was weather-reactive. From this unimpeachable source it followed that all weather predictions could be made without fear. To add to this conviction, above this scientific *objét* was screwed a small, neatly executed notice. This read 'In God we Trust.' Clearly our boffins considered it worth covering all their bases.

It was here that Ted Wilkins and his team worked under the supervision of the Senior Meteorological Officer, Bill Collins. Their chief tasks were the plotting of our six-hourly balloon and radio-sonde flights from the data fed them from the Radar Control Office, the acquisition of all manner of other meteorological data and the consequent compilation of synoptic charts.

Fitted with a fine-meshed radar reflector, the passage of the balloon and its dependant kit revealed the speeds and directions of upper atmosphere winds, while the little radio-sonde – a clever, cheap and expendable device – transmitted the basic data of atmospheric pressure, temperature and relative humidity as the balloon ascended. Some of these balloon flights were notable for their duration and the altitude reached, occasionally over 110,000 feet, well into the stratosphere. In terms of distance they commonly disappeared down-wind beyond the scope of the big Type 244 radar to follow them but they might go on for some hours after the initial launch.

The whole contraption fell back into the sea when the expansion of the balloon, huge by this time, had passed the limits of its elasticity and was so thin that it burst. But they sometimes descended upon land, where, thanks to the deployment of a small parachute to minimise damage, they might be discovered and recovered. The Meteorological Office offered the generous reward of ten shillings for any radio-sonde returned to them.

Incidentally, just as the sailors and the engine-room staff were recruited locally and were thus Scottish to a man, because the Headquarters of the British Meteorological Office was at

Bracknell in Berkshire and all the members of the Met. Department were career meteorologists, they consisted almost entirely of Englishmen. In similar vein, since the Met. Office was an off-shoot of what was then the Air Ministry, most of the radar operatives were ex-Royal Air Force personnel. And while I'm on the subject of crew, I should perhaps explain that the deck-officers, like myself, all had our roots in the Merchant Navy, generally- speaking that is, though there was the occasional anomaly. Thus it was that we three bridge watch-keeping officers, plus Captain Gordon, all held standard mercantile Ministry of Transport Certificates of Competency.

But to revert to the ship's layout. Abutting the after bulkhead of the Met. Office rose the hideous yet essential structure of the balloon hangar. Its after end was open and from under its roof hung a sort of inverted cone. On either side of the exterior of the hangar and along those of the Met. Office were rows of gas accumulators, red bottles, each of which was charged with hydrogen under pressure. In short, the after quarter of the *Weather Guardian* was a floating bomb. When on our weather 'station,' every six hours, a balloon was filled with hydrogen and the ship was brought head to wind, preparatory to a launch. In order for this process to be accomplished, first the balloon was held under the inverted cone where the gas was fed into it until it was about two metres in diameter and lightly 'jammed' itself into the cone, the head of which was flexible. The radar-reflector and radio-sonde were then secured to the closed-off neck of the balloon underneath. Two of the Met. Assistants then pulled the balloon out of the cone, clinging on to it to resist its desire to rise. They then dragged it clear of the hangar and let go, with a mutual shout of 'Balloon's away!' This message was picked up on the bridge and in the Radar Control Room where there was a brief hiatus until the word was passed that the 'target' had been acquired. Thereafter the ascent proceeded as I have already outlined.

So there she lay, across the dock, her grey hull topped with this jumble of light-orange superstructures and, I should add, sundry antennae poking up into the sky from sundry locations along her upper-works and masts, an ugly-duck of a British Ocean Weather Ship.

Having taken a couple of photographs I walked back to her gangway, first coming abreast of her flared bow with its bar-stem, sharp rake and the very obvious signs of hard service. It has to be said that she was stouter than many an all-welded modern frigate, where the joining intersection of frames, inter-costals, stringers and decks produces the dimpled effect likened to a 'hungry-horse'. Nevertheless, the *Weather Guardian*'s shell plating bore a good few indentations and a number of rusty streaks. Behind those battered plates, in the body of the hull, the majority of the crew, including the officers like myself, slept and messed. My own cabin lay on the port side, just abaft the old trunking that supported the gun, so I was situated quite far forward and my single cabin port-hole was no more than about eight feet above the waterline. It was well dogged-down and, in really rough weather, further covered by a steel dead-light, otherwise, when the ship rolled, I could alternately observe the sky or gaze down into the deep, deep sea.

At the foot of the gangway I worked my way through half-a-dozen vehicles, mostly delivery vans, but a couple of private cars, as we took aboard our victuals and other stores and chandlery. Iain Mackenzie was on deck at the top of the gangway, talking some matter over with the Bosun, a softly spoken Tuchter from Stornoway and both men nodded at me as I passed. Dropping my camera off in my cabin, I collected my sextant box, volume of Norie's Nautical Tables and my manuscript sight-book and made my way up to the navigating bridge, intending to stow them in the cubby hole provided. To get there I had to pass through the Captain's flat. His cabin door was open, though the curtain was drawn and I could hear voices. One was a woman's and I recalled passing the Old Man's Ford car on the quay. Mrs Gordon had come to see her husband safely aboard and settled-in.

I passed on up to the flat accommodating the Comms. and Radar Offices and, tucking my books under my arm, swung myself onto the vertical ladder that led up, through a water-tight hatch to the wheelhouse, aware that a loud and stentorian voice was singing above me, belting out 'Bless your beautiful hide!' from the musical film *Seven Brides for Seven Brothers*. It took me a second clamber to haul up my sextant box, whereupon I recovered the books from the deck beside the hatch coaming and made for the entrance to the chart-room.

In the wheelhouse one of the able-seamen, McGrigor I think it was, was buffing-up the bridge brass. He was tight-lipped, though he acknowledged my arrival with a brief 'Mornin,' sir,' rolling his eyes in the direction of the chart-room. Just as I approached the entrance I found it blocked by a large, stocky, full-bearded figure of a man wearing the dark blue trousers and battle-dress that was our sea-going rig. On his head he wore a cockily angled blue beret with the badge of the Ocean Weather Service neatly sewn on.

His shoulder-boards were identical to mine, but he was at least twice my age and probably more, fifty plus to my twenty-two, grizzled and with a shock of grey hair. What skin of his face was visible above his formidable beard was weather-beaten and wrinkled. Set in deep sockets a pair of grey eyes glared at me. Our confrontation had abruptly cut his musical output.

'And who have we here?' he boomed inquisitively, as if my intrusion was an unwelcome interruption of his choral exhibition.

I put the sextant box on the deck for the second time and held out my right hand.

'James Childe, Third Officer,' I said rather warily, for if this was our new Acting Second Officer he was not at all what I had expected.

He ignored my outstretched hand.

'James Child, eh? And a fellow Southeran, thank God! What fate drew you to the benighted shores of the Clyde, eh? I'm Charles Pennington, *Acting* Second Officer,' he rumbled on without waiting for any response from me (I dropped my hand at this point), but with heavy emphasis on his temporary status. 'Well Child James,' he said flippantly, 'do you like to be called James, Jim, Jimmy, or – given *oor'* (this with much phonetic exaggeration) 'present location - *wee Jamie*?'

I smiled. 'I haven't had much choice in the matter,' I replied, 'but Jamie seems to be the norm hereabouts.'

'Quite right too,' Pennington responded. 'And I'm Charles, not Chas, or, God forbid, Charlie.' He paused, as if willing me to take note of this as an instruction, then repeated, '*never* Charlie.' I thought for a moment that his eyes hardened.

'Now tell me, what Certificate of Competence do you hold?' he asked, following it up with a question as to my previous experience.

I told him that I held a First Mate's Certificate and where I had been since coming to sea, all of which he digested before remarking in an extremely facetious manner, 'Well I hope, wee Jamie, you are not one of those deck ornaments that is all piss, epaulettes and importance with no *bottom* – and I do not mean that last in either the anatomical or the nautical sense but that archaic form denoting gravitas.' He did not wait for me to respond to this fatuity but continued his interrogation. 'And how many trips have you done in this rust-bucket?'

'Three,' I said, tamping down a strange and unwarranted compulsion to add 'sir,' which was entirely unnecessary but seemed the best way of containing my rising temper. I had stood this sort of crap from senior officers before. I had to remind myself that he was barely my senior; it was an aggravating situation in which to find myself.

'*Three*, Child James, *three*,' Pennington said with an affected air of wonder, throwing the information out to the wider world. 'Why that's two more than most lads of your age to be sure. Well, well; I suppose we must consider that to your credit in one way. Most of them chuck it in after the first. On the other hand, they say that if you do more than *three* voyages you never leave.'

'So I've heard,' I responded drily, 'but I have plans and have no intention of remaining here for much longer.'

'Is that so? And does your future plan mind you being away for Christmas in this Year of Our Lord nineteen hundred and sixty six, Child James?'

I confess to being a little non-plussed by the directness and intimacy of this question. But it was not one I could dodge without being rude. Besides, I was still under that odd compulsion to address my interlocutor as 'sir,' even though I was tiring of his disregard of my desire to be called 'Jamie' and rapidly losing any inherent respect I might have had for him.

'Yes, of course she does,' I retorted rather sharply.

'Well, well.'

Somehow - I'm not quite sure how and perhaps it was only an after-thought - but I sensed he acknowledged the spirit in my retort. But I do recall that Pennington drew his head back and regarded me rather archly, shooting a glance at Able-seaman McGrigor who, apart from rubbing the boss at the centre of the ship's wheel, was listening with a rapt intent to our little cabaret act. (God alone knows how he would relate it to his mess-mates at dinner.) I thought he was turning his attention thither, but Pennington had not yet finished with me.

'Well Child James, we shall see, we shall see. As the Yankee poet Emerson sagaciously wrote, "Things are in the saddle, and ride mankind." '

I was not certain what to make of this portentous utterance, but it was clear that I was being taken the measure of, guyed if not actually goaded. Although I had no problem with a little light chi-iking, such as I had endured at the hands of Iain Mackenzie and Dougal Henty the previous day, there was something verging on the unpleasant about this first encounter with Pennington. I couldn't immediately lay my finger on it, but later in the day, when thinking it over, I nailed it down to the empowered superiority of an English public-school education. The fellow's natural accent suggested this to be the case and I had encountered such a thing on two previous occasions, but from younger men nearer my own age. Besides, the point seemed over-heavily made for a man of fifty or so whose schooling was long past. All I knew in that moment was that, fifty or not, I must lay down my marker.

'I'm James Childe,' I said firmly, 'Childe with an 'e' and not – *never* - Child James, if you please! And how many trips have *you* done in these vessels?'

He appeared to glare at me and then he smiled, at least I think he smiled, for it was difficult to see his mouth under the huge full-set of a beard, but his grey eyes twinkled. '*Touché*, my friend, *touché*,' he said, thrusting out a huge paw.

I shook hands. His grip was firm but not over-whelming; moreover, he had turned his head and seemed to me to gaze wistfully out of the wheel-house windows to the snow-covered hills of distant Dumbarton and Argyll across the firth. 'As to how many trips I have done, I've lost count… How many is it Archie?' he called out to the able-seaman.

'I dinna ken, sir,' replied McGrigor, polishing industriously. 'Ah've sailed with ye maybe ten oor a dozen times mebbe, though not always on the same ship. You come and go a wee bit… I canna keep track…'

'Aye,' said Pennington ruminatively, 'I come and go…quite a lot actually,' this last was uttered as he turned back to me. 'Yes, quite a lot. You see, Jamie, an ocean wanderer can always find a berth in these little rust-buckets… that's the beauty of them!'

Then, seeing the bundle of books under my left arm, he made way for me to enter the chart-room. 'Oh, please, come and stow your stuff on your shelf…'

The tone of his voice and his demeanour had changed in the twinkling of an eye to that of a sudden charming colleague.

And that is how I met Charles Pennington, Acting Second Officer of the Ocean Weather Ship *Weather Guardian* in December 1966.

*

As we were sailing on the high-water at 13.00 I got into the wardroom early, ready to sit down for my dinner at noon sharp. The ship was now buzzing with life and smells. The boilers were cooking up steam ready for our departure and hot-water had been running throughout the central heating system long enough now to make the internal spaces of the ship warm and even cosy.

The Old Man's wife had departed in her car and I had caught one glimpse of Captain Gordon, a pleasant West Highland man – what one might described with perfect accuracy as 'a tall raw-boned Scot'. I had got on with him very well on our previous voyages together and he was a first-class seaman, an excellent commander who was happy to delegate to his officers once they had gained his trust. Thus it was that 'on station manoeuvring' was often left up to the Officer-of-the-Watch, something I had never experienced in cargo-liners. There were some things he had to be on the bridge for, such as to relieve me when, about once a week when we were on station, I had to take a plankton haul and preserve the specimens I caught in my net, ready to send off at the end of every voyage to the laboratories of the Ministry of Agriculture and Fisheries, near Lowestoft. He would also be in charge when we carried out an exercise with the Royal Air Force, or when we did a full air-sea rescue evolution, or any other drill such as our regular fire and lifeboat practice, when all the officers were deployed on various duties. But most of the time, though he would often put in a supervisory appearance when some routine evolution was under-way, he commanded with a light touch.

He did like a yarn, though, often remaining on the bridge with me for an hour after I had taken a plankton haul, and he was a great raconteur, both in respect of his own experiences, which had begun when he had gone to sea as a boy, long before the Second World War, but also about Scottish history, for which he had a deep love.

I was the first officer into the wardroom and instead of taking my seat at one of the two long tables I wandered over to the after bulkhead where, beside the door to the pantry, an oil painting of the ship hung.

Painted by a previous Third Officer, it depicted a starboard-side view of the *Weather Guardian* plunging into a big head sea. Heavy roiling clouds streamed downwind and, on her rising stern, three or four dabs of paint indicated two Met. Assistants who had just released a radio-sonde balloon which was ascending into the air astern of the ship. The ship's big tracking scanner was trained aft and a few more dabs of oil-paint showed the Officer-of the Watch observing the release of the balloon.

It was quite competently done for an amateur effort; the sea and the sky were lively, the detail of the ship was well-wrought, and I rather liked it. It had an especial attraction for me because, in the foreground under the starboard bow, two starkly black and white killer whales leapt out of the water. It reminded me of the painting seen by Ishmael hanging on the wall of the Spouter's Inn in an early chapter of Melville's great story, *Moby Dick*. Not literally, of course, for the cetacean there was a mighty sperm whale and it was leaping clear over the whaling ship sent out to hunt for him, but in a subtler manner.

One of my ancillary duties was to collect and collate any reported sighting of cetaceans – whales, dolphins and the like, and in three voyages I had managed a mere five sightings of schools of pilot whales. It was a rather depressing total and every time I had joined the ship and seen the painting I revived my hope of seeing something more dramatic than these rather common 'black-fish'.

A pod of Orca would do very nicely thank you, or one of the larger species of baleen whales such as a big rorqual like a Minke, or better still a hump-back. Yes, a hump-back would put icing on the cake of my desire. Anyway, as I stood there the steward announced dinner was ready, and just as I was taking my seat, Ted Wilkins came in with his boss, the Senior Met. Officer, Bill Collins, followed by the Captain. Within two or three minutes the place was full, unusually full, for once at sea roughly half of us would be on watch and we would eat by sittings. The total complement of officers was, besides the Captain, we three deck, or navigating, officers; the chief and three engineer officers, two electronic officers, two communications officers, an electrical officer and two meteorological officers, plus a chief and second steward who usually ate in the chief's cabin where, it was credibly whispered, they did rather better for grub than the rest of us.

The rest of our ship's company, the seamen and deck-boys led by the Bosun, the firemen and greasers who manned the combined boiler-room and engine room, the meteorological., communications and electronics personnel, plus our cooks and the saloon steward, had their own mess-rooms, some of them – the specialist 'assistants' – ranking as petty-officers. A relaxed form of naval-style working uniform was worn by all petty-officers and ratings, known as Number 8's for the naval buffs, drawn from the Base stores at Greenock. As I have previously mentioned, all officers wore battle-dress, usually with a beret, though we were supposed to carry caps and reefers. One or two of our engineers favoured the high-necked patrol jackets long out of favour elsewhere.

So there you have us all – ship and crew - in the mind's eye, immediately before our departure of the forty-third voyage of the Ocean Weather Ship *Weather Guardian* from her Base at Greenock into the grim, grey wastes of a wintry North Atlantic.

*

Half an hour later the ward-room was empty, except for the saloon steward who was busy clearing the tables, and at 12.50 the hands were called to 'stations' for leaving harbour. My post for this was on the bridge, with the Old Man and fifteen minutes after he had given the order to 'let-go!' I had rung on the engines to full speed as, having cleared the dock entrance, we headed for Loch Striven.

It was a bitterly cold but beautiful afternoon, with the snow bright upon the mountains and the Firth of Clyde blue with that hue that bespeaks a numbing chill. The westerly wind could be seen blowing snow off the summits of the Argyll highlands as we passed Gourock to port and to starboard, the Holy Loch. This short inlet was occupied by the huge grey submarine depot-ship of the United States Navy, alongside which a brace of evil-looking black nuclear-powered and nuclear-armed American submarines lay, recuperating between patrols. The Cold War was still then a dominating factor in world affairs and we all existed under the threat of mutual destruction in the apparently insoluble stand-off between the NATO powers led by the

United States and those of the Warsaw Pact, led by the Union of Soviet Socialist Republics. It gave the name of the loch a decidedly hollow ring.

As we passed the Holy Loch, Pennington, who had come up from his station down aft, picked up a pair of the powerful Barr & Stroud binoculars that we had deployed in boxes about the wheelhouse and went out onto the exposed bridge-wing. For some time he stared at the American warships, an action, I noticed, that drew the attention of both Captain Gordon and Iain Mackenzie, who had also come up on the bridge after securing the forecastle-head. The two men exchanged glances. I did not attach much importance to this at the time, being busy with my own duties, which were to plot the ship's position every ten minutes as we proceeded down the firth and advise the Old Man if we were deviating from the course line. (We would not go into sea-watches until after we had left Loch Striven, so the Old Man had the con.)

By the time Pennington eventually came back into the wheelhouse we had passed Between Cloch Point and Dunoon, and the entrance to the Holy Loch had shut in. The Second Officer brought into the warm wheelhouse an icy blast and, having returned the big pair of glasses into their teak box, rubbed his cold hands together. His eyes were full of tears, I assumed from the cold, his cheeks were wet and the moisture had actually frozen on the grey moustache of his full set.

He caught my eye and grinned. 'Freeze the bollocks off a brass monkey,' he murmured, following me into the chart-room where he watched as I laid the ship's position down.

Captain Gordon stayed on the bridge for the short passage of a couple of hours round Toward Point and then north, into Loch Striven. Here, at about four o'clock, we ran alongside and secured to the NATO fuelling station, the tanks of which were buried in the hillside at the root of the short pier. Over the following couple of hours, we filled our guts with boiler-oil before we finally cast off and headed for the Atlantic.

The outer Firth of Clyde is an immense body of water. It took us some hours to run southwards down its length until, passing the island of Pladda, off the far larger Isle of Arran, we altered course to the south-west. Later, off the island of Sanda, we began rounding the Mull of Kintyre, swinging all the time further to the westward until, around midnight, as I handed over the watch to Pennington, we were on a roughly north-westerly course for the open ocean.

By this time we were heading into a north-north-westerly gale, a full Force 8 on the Beaufort scale, our speed down to about 8 knots and the ship pitching into a heavy wind-sea and an under-lying heavy swell. The sky was now completely overcast. As the handful of shore lights fell astern and disappeared, I wondered if any Soviet Russian submarines had seen us. Passing through these waters on previous voyages we had observed periscopes, the forward eyes of the *Tovarisches* keeping an eye on the gateway not only to the Yanks' submarine movements in-and-out of the Holy Loch, but our own British 'boats' operating from Faslane.

After the humiliation of the climb-down by Soviet forces – and particularly their submarines – during the Cuban missile crisis of 'sixty-two, Admiral Sergei Gorshkov had patiently built-up a formidable surface and sub-surface naval force in the Soviet Northern Fleet. At that time it was not therefore uncommon to see one of their boat's periscopes, often, I used to think, deployed just to be seen and to taunt us. What the Russians thought of our old fashioned jumbled-up rust-buckets as we battered our way out to our lonely stations, I have no idea, but their presence, or even the notion of their presence, with their noses poked into our waters, undoubtedly had an intimidating effect. It reminded us that we were on our own.

Very much on our own.

It is fair to say, and in the light of the ensuing events, important, not merely to say but to emphasise, that the foulness of the weather notwithstanding, the duties of an Ocean Weather Ship and her crew were pretty boring. Certainly there was a routine to it all, but after a few days the routine grew dull, along with the food and a good deal of the company. This is not a reflection on the character of individuals, but of the monotony – the same faces, the same dull diet, the same sea, the same sky, and the endless motion of the ship. I shall come to this last later; the point I wish to make here is that no-one was on board to enjoy the life on the ocean wave. Not at all; they were there because the leave was good and they weren't away from home longer than thirty–odd days, with exactly twenty-eight on station. Moreover, in order to get one's full allocation of leave in, one could, every now and again, take a voyage off.

Nevertheless, thirty days could seem an eternity, especially to the younger men, particularly on the northerly weather stations, of which INDIA was one. In such circumstances small irritations could blow-up into grievances and it was a small tribute to the stoicism of the men who manned these lonely vessels that these circumstances did not lead to more than the odd quarrel – invariably among the youngsters – when a dose of cabin-fever over-heated. Only an eccentric with his own personal reasons for doing so could come anywhere near enjoying a routine voyage in an Ocean Weather Ship.

Our employers were well aware of this – hence the generous leave and the odd voyage off. We were also sent to sea with a selection of films, usually two a week and shown in the petty-officer's mess, part of the largesse allowed British armed forces to counter *ennui*. We were also permitted a small daily allowance of alcohol, a couple of cans of beer, I seem to recall, with the officers allowed to exchange a beer for a tiny measure of spirits. Needless to say, although it was against regulations, we used to hoard our allowance and enjoy a so-called 'party' on Saturday nights. These were held in various parts of the ship; I used to join the group that met in the Chief Steward's cabin, which was not far from my own. Apart from enjoying a few beers, our conversation often ran deep, for we were all philosophers of one kind or another. Moreover, thanks to our varied backgrounds, we all brought differing perspectives to our gatherings.

So, although it might justifiably be said that life aboard was unpleasant and routinely dull, there were a few compensations.

And that first night at sea we had no reason whatsoever to assume that the voyage upon which we had now embarked would be anything other than just that. A period of time to be endured and little more.

2

As Third Mate I kept the eight-to-twelve watch, morning and evening. Irrespective of our western longitude, the ship's time conformed to what was still then called Greenwich Mean Time. This meant that when the sky was clear enough I took solar observations during the forenoon and stellar sights in the early evening. Since the necessary conditions for astro-navigation were rare in the North Atlantic, especially in winter, we were fitted with LORAN, Long Range Navigation, a radio-wave based system dating – like the receiver from which we extracted the data – of Second World War vintage. It was pretty accurate on Ocean Station INDIA, so our sun and star sights were checks, important checks nonetheless, which also kept out hands in at our ancient craft. The importance of knowing exactly where we were will be made clearer shortly but on that outward passage to Ocean Station INDIA we operated like any other vessel on passage. There were no Saturday night 'parties,' or other homespun distractions; these were reserved for our four weeks 'on station'.

Naturally that first night at sea we all slept badly – in fact we rarely slept well at all, which was one of our existential problems – but one tended to get used to a lack of shut-eye just as one got used to the eternal rolling and pitching of the ship, even though the debilitating effects ground one down. Anyway, when I climbed up to the bridge the following morning the gale had increased to Force 9, a 'strong gale' on Admiral Francis

Beaufort's scale, and we were down to about 7.5 knots. With the wind on our port bow we were pitching heavily into a head sea, but were rolling too, a cork-screwing motion that soon sorted the men from the boys where sea-sickness was concerned. All of the five ship's boys, those employed on deck, in the galley and in the mess-decks, suffered, but so too did a number of the older men. Some of the 'specialists sat at their stations, be they Radio Comms, Radar, or Met, with buckets between their legs, at least for the first few days.

Besides the wind and sea we were now treated to rain squalls, which severely limited visibility but all of which we took in our stride as we banged and bashed our way to windward. Two days out we passed the lonely sea-mount of Rockall, a black triangle of rock against which the Western Ocean battered. The monolith stood not so much a reminder of land, but of the remoteness of our eventual destination, which was not far distant. The weather had cleared a little and the wind dropped a tad, so a few fulmar petrels swept around the ship on their sabre-like wings, like small northern albatrosses. Gannets – or Solan geese as the Scots called them – were also in evidence and at lunch that day Ted Wilkins told me that some tiny, dark stormy petrels had been reported hunting in the ship's wake by one of the Met. Assistants who had ventured onto the after deck in quest of a photograph of the ship in heavy weather.

At noon I handed over to Pennington, went below for my dinner and then turned-in. In weather such as we were then experiencing, one's bunk was the only refuge. One didn't have to sleep – though eventually one almost always drifted off for a while – but one could enjoy a good read. I always took a small selection of reading matter. That trip, I remember, I had a copy of Cook's *Voyages*, *Gulliver's Travels* and the short stories of 'Saki'.

By 20.00 that evening I was back on watch and for three hours

I kept my vigil with Able-seaman Archie McGrigor and a first-trip Deck Boy named Hamish Davison. Hamish, as we all called him, had a shock of red hair, a face full of freckles and the lean look of a lad from Glasgow's less salubrious parts. At this stage in the trip he was quiet, half terrified by the ship's motion and half by sea-sickness. They say there are two stages to this malaise; the first is that you think that you are going to die, the second that you profoundly hope that you will, and soon. Thereafter, except in rare cases, you recover. Hamish would recover in full.

Towards the end of the watch, things began to liven up. The heavy swell remained, but the wind-sea, now under the influence of a Force 6, had dropped markedly as we approached the south-east corner of the grid marking on our plotting charts the extent of Ocean Station INDIA.

This grid needs some explanation. It was a notion taken directly from the location system used by Admiral Dönitz's U-boats in the Second World War, only instead of covering the entire North Atlantic, each of the four ocean weather stations manned in turn by Great Britain, France, The Netherlands and Norway was composed of a single grid 210 miles square.

Our actual internationally recognised 'on station' position – officially known as *Oscar Sierra* according to the international phonetic alphabet - was a ten-nautical mile square the centre of which for O.S INDIA was at Latitude 59° 00' North, and Longitude 19° 30' West. This point on the surface of the globe lay at the centre of a ten mile square, and stretching out to the north, south, east and west for 100 miles in each direction, lay other 10 miles squares, each with a two-letter designation, making a grid 210 miles by 210 miles. Under all reasonable conditions, we were supposed to remain within the 10 mile boundaries of *Oscar Sierra*, but in heavy weather we were allowed to drift up to 20 miles to leeward of O.S. before making our way back, usually to 20 miles upwind of O.S. so that the whole cycle could repeat itself.

Only in exceptional circumstances were we permitted to venture farther off into the outer limits of the grid, but it was there for a reason. We were not on station just to collect meteorological and oceanographical data (which I shall have more to say later), we were also there to render assistance, particularly to trans-Atlantic aircraft. These took all forms: military flights, the delivery flights of sometimes quite small commercial aeroplanes manufactured in the United States and on their way to a European destination, and trans-Atlantic passenger air-liners. Should any one of these, but especially the last, get into trouble, they could make for our grid and ditch alongside us. To help them we could move towards them, even if in an extreme situation it meant leaving our 'box'.

In support of aviation generally we acted as a radio-beacon, a supplementary aid to aircraft navigation – which was still in those days not much more sophisticated than the surface navigation we used at sea. When in our central square the Comms. Station blasted out into the aether from an aerial array between our two masts, our designation of INDIA, followed by the two-letter grid-square we then occupied – normally, of course, O.S. If we moved out of this, as for example having been blown to leeward, this would change to the appropriate two-letters designating our 'new' grid square.

It was part of the job of our three navigating officers to keep the Comms. Team updated on our current two-letter grid reference so that our transmitted radio-beacon transmission was correct. In these days of geostationary satellite navigational systems accurate to fractions of a metre, sending out a signal covering a 10 miles square may seem less than helpful, but in 1966, this remained far from the case, especially in the case of smaller aircraft some of which were flown by solo pilots. To better gauge such matters, it is worth pointing out that, at the time a skilful astro-navigator, with clear visibility and a good horizon who took a clear set of stellar observations could be pleased with a result that gave him a good outcome, but he would never claim it to be more accurate than to the margin of two nautical miles. Out in the Western Ocean such an accuracy was good enough.

Now, the purpose of all this is to explain that at about 23.00 that night, as my watch was drawing towards its end we were closing the south-east corner of Ocean Station INDIA's grid. To facilitate a crisp changeover, all weather ships were allowed to leave their OS position and work their way down to this corner square (adjusting their radio-beacon signal accordingly) where the on-coming duty vessel would make a rendezvous and pick-up the duty of being Ocean Station INDIA.

And that is what happened at midnight that night.

Shortly before 23.00 I had bridge-to-bridge VHF radio-telephone contact with the Dutch OWS *Stratus* – a converted former American destroyer-escort.

A little later Captain Gordon joined me on the bridge and, after a cordial exchange of greetings, during which the official time of hand-over was agreed between us, the *Weather Guardian* metamorphosed into Ocean Station INDIA. Less formally, and with detectable glee, the *Stratus* wished us a happy Christmas before speeding off on her way back toward Rotterdam with a following wind and sea. For our part we took up the mantle of duty and immediately began broadcasting our changing two-letter designation as, at 10 knots or so – the wind having dropped further – we ploughed our way towards the centre of our grid.

Although at least another ten hours would elapse before we reached our final destination, our routine was no longer that of a vessel on passage. Everything now underwent a shift in gear and the first movement fell upon Charles Pennington's shoulders as he took over the twelve-to-four. Having seen the Second Officer and his watch-keepers settled-in, both Captain Gordon and I went below to our respective bunks. I think I probably sat up for twenty minutes to write up my private Journal before I 'crashed,' jamming myself into my bunk, to read until Saki sent me to sleep.

*

The *Weather Guardian* reached Ocean Station INDIA at 10.12 the following forenoon, roughly half-way through my morning watch. The west south-westerly wind had dropped to about Force 5/6 – a strong breezes – which blew over a bleak grey-blue sea, reflecting a lowering overcast out of which a periodic snow squall swept towards us and across our upper-deck. Although the wind-sea had fallen away significantly, the oceanic ground-swell remained heavy, verging on the very heavy, and we continued to roll, but mostly pitch.

I informed Captain Gordon, the Met. Office and the Comms. staff – who adjusted our radio-beacon signal accordingly. The Old Man came up on the bridge. Checked the position and joined me in the wheelhouse where I took my own station close to our navigating radar and keeping an eye on the ship's head and oncoming seas. Morning coffee had just arrived and he and I stood, side-by-side, sipping from our big mugs and studying the bleak prospect ahead of us. I knew what was coming.

'We'll carry on fur another ten miles then lie a-hull,' Captain Gordon ordered quietly.

'Aye. Aye, sir,' I responded. Although we only flashed-up the second boiler in an emergency, Gordon was still under a standing order to conserve fuel and it was not necessary to heave the ship-to, head to sea unless the weather was extreme. We would therefore steam into the wind a further 10 miles, then stop the engines and lie beam-on – or a-hull – to the wind and sea and drift to leeward until 10 miles beyond O.S. when we would get under way, steam to windward for 20 miles and repeat the process. Naturally, if the weather became intolerable we would heave-to, but it was customary to ly a-hull in winds in excess of gale force, and to drift to leeward at up to a surprising 4 knots. And of course, this drifting would be interrupted by the necessity to come up into the wind for the balloon launches at noon, 18.00, midnight and 06.00.

'Keep her head to wind until after the noon balloon flight,' Gordon added. 'Just slow her doon.'

'Aye. Aye, sir,' I repeated. In addition to the engine-room telegraph by which means we signalled our requirements to the engine room – full, half, slow and dead slow, both a head and astern, plus stand-by and finished with engines – we retained an ex-warship's refinement of being able to 'ring on' or take off a few revs. at a time by means of a small controller on the forward bulkhead in the wheelhouse. This was used a lot in heavy weather, and kept the unfortunate duty engineer down below as busy as a dancing flea. It was a good idea to get on socially with one's colleague in 'the black pit.' Happily in my case this was Fourth Engineer Colin Buchanan, a good tempered Clyde-sider.

'And then you can lay her a-hull.' And with that the Old Man left me to it. Unless he was in one of his chatty moods, which usually occurred in the evenings, Captain Gordon was a man of few words.

It was one of the misfortunes of being Third Officer that one did half an hour's extra duty in the morning watch, allowing the Second Officer to eat his dinner at noon and repair to the bridge at 12.30. It was a small compensation for his having his sleep interrupted by the midnight to 04.00 'grave-yard' watch, but a large imposition on me. I didn't really resent it, but after the balloon launch, spot on noon, the last twenty-five or so minutes used to drag appallingly.

Not that it bothered me that first morning; one had to get back into the swing of things and although we had been launching our balloon ever since we relieved the *Stratus*, this would be the first time this trip that we carried out a major manoeuvre afterwards. I don't want to make out that this manoeuvre amounted to very much, but it altered everything.

After we had watched the pale globe of the balloon and its dependant instruments disappear astern into the scud and received confirmation from the main tracking radar that they had 'acquired' it, I made a preliminary phone call to the engine room then made an announcement over the ship's public address system prior to carrying out Captain Gordon's last order.

'Attention! Attention! Officer-of the-Watch speaking. We will shortly be swinging beam-on. Please secure all loose gear.' This last was to warn anyone who had left personal items sculling about in their cabins that unless they were tucked away somewhere safe, they could look for them on the deck. It was also to warn the Cooks who, although they used 'fiddles' on the galley stove, stood in mortal danger of a good scalding. After a few minutes, I ordered the helm put over to port and rang 'Stop,' on the engine-room telegraph. The *Weather Guardian* fell off the wind to port, her pitching eased and she began to roll like the devil, simultaneously rising and falling as the heavy swell passed under her.

''Midships.'

''Midships, sir...wheel's amindships.'

The wheel was secured by a rope becket and McGrigor, being the good seaman that he was, began to busy himself tidying up the wheel-house, emptying the ash-trays and so forth, before starting on the brass-work. Hamish, on the other hand, stood about idly and I watched him for a moment before crossing to the port side and opening the leeward wheel-house door.

Turning back to the deck-boy I jerked my head.

'Out on the bridge wing, son, and keep a lookout.' Hamish glared at me incredulously, but McGrigor made a sort of ruminative noise, which propelled the lad through the open door as a shot from a gun. As he passed me, he gave me a baleful stare. I went to the forward wheelhouse windows to take a look round while behind me, McGrigor shut the wheel-house door.

I turned round and found the Able-seaman grinning at me. 'He's got tae learn, sir,' he said simply, resuming his polishing.

Shortly afterwards, with a chorus of *Men of Harlech*, Pennington emerged through the wheel-house hatch. After a few moments handing over, during which McGrigor and Hamish also turned their duties over to their reliefs, Pennington and I stood quietly staring at the desolation of sea; *Weather Guardian* was now rolling through about seventy or eighty degrees, the fulmars swooping about her on their long, elegant glides, their motionless wing-tips coming within a few centimetres of the sea's surface.

'No kittiwakes,' remarked Pennington, adding peremptorily, 'enjoy your lunch.'

I was dismissed. Once again, I got that sensation that I was very inferior to him in moral rank, if not the actual. It was unsettling, but I left him to it without another word.

*

I am sorry that I have had to dwell a good deal on the technical side of things, but I hope you will realise in due course that all this is necessary to give you some idea of the curious life we led out there on the bosom of the Western Ocean. There will, moreover, be a bit more, but we can wait until it fits the narrative.

For the time being we had settled into our 'on station' routine and events would roll-out accordingly for a while. I was relieved at midnight and 12.30 by Pennington, who handed over to Iain Mackenzie at 16.00 and 04.00, whom I relieved at 20.00 and 08.00. Balloon flights therefore took place in Iain and my watches. Other activities could occur according to either Captain Gordon's orders, or special instructions received from the Met. Office at Bracknell via Portishead Radio, the major British long-range radio station located near Bristol for all commercial and non-military radio traffic. Here a special 'desk' dealt with communications with us and our fellows to the north and south of INDIA.

For a couple of days nothing much happened until our first Friday on station when I made my first plankton haul. As I have mentioned, this meant that Captain Gordon relieved me on the bridge and I took McGrigor with me to the special winch down aft and dropped my small, fine-meshed trawl over the side. The job had to be done during the hours of darkness when the tiny creatures had risen towards the surface and the contents of the net were transferred into special jars containing formalin. A note of the date, time and our position was made on the jar's label. The whole task took about forty minutes; it was usually a cold, wet and miserable duty, carried out largely by torch-light on a deck slippery with deposited spray and rolling like a bastard. One's bare hands, to say nothing of one's nose, were cut by the wind and we were glad to get back to the steam-heated cocoon of the wheel-house where McGrigor made hot, sweet tea or cocoa.

The evening of that first plankton haul Captain Gordon was not only in the mood to talk, he had something rather more than our usual chit-chat. He sat on the chart-room settee under the red chart-room lamps while I warmed-up, drank my tea and kept an eye on the radar. I left the visual lookout to McGrigor and Hamish whom the Able-seaman had taken under his wing with a view to 'brining the wee laddie on'. Before the end of the voyage we hoped he would become a competent helmsman, but that depended upon us being underway and not lying a-hull, and that night we were lying a-hull.

'Ah'm sorry,' began Gordon, 'that ye didna sail this trip as Acting Second Mate, Jamie,' he said, using the old rank favoured by many hard-case former mercantile officers.

'That's okay, sir,' I responded, but the matter was troubling the Old Man.

He scratched his head, 'Ah did tell the Base Captain that you were likely to leave the Sairvice withoout a bit o' encouragement and that Davie having gone sick offered you such an opportunity.' He sighed, took a gulp of his tea, and went on, 'but the auld bugger told me he wanted a berth for Pennington, so that was that. As Ah say, Ah'm sorry.'

I frowned. As I have mentioned, I had no intention of staying in the Service, but I had had a series of unfortunate circumstances blight my promotional prospects in my earlier career, for none of which I was responsible, I might add. Nevertheless, as I mentioned earlier, I would have seized the chance of having a shot at the higher rank. On the other hand I had no right to make a fuss, but what Gordon had just told me was at variance with what Iain Mackenzie had said the afternoon I joined the ship.

'I thought the Second Officer was transferred from the *Weather Follower*, sir,' I said.

Captain Gordon looked at me a bit oddly, frowned himself and shook his head. 'No, no,' he said, 'Captain Brownhall employs him frae time-tae time...'

Brownhall was the Base Captain, what in a commercial shipping company would be called a Marine Superintendent. Having risen to command a corvette in the war, when peace came he was appointed to one of the first of the British Ocean Weather Ships – the old Flower-class corvettes – that initiated the post-war Ocean Weather Service. He was, in effect, our –

and Gordon's – boss, the manager of the four British Ocean Weather Ships based at Greenock. He was a formidable character who, despite his small stature, cut a fine figure behind his desk, dressed in his full reefers, his right-breast bearing an impressive row of medal ribbons, including that of the Distinguished Service Cross. The keen-eyed noticed this had a bar; 'Bullshit Brownhall,' as he was irreverently known, had been a U-boat killer, and one suspected that his life thereafter had been something of an anti-climax.

'Oh well,' I said with perhaps a tad of injudicious inflection, 'if he's one of Captain Brownhall's favourites, I'm not the man to argue.'

'Huh,' Gordon grunted. 'Ah'm not sae sure, but Ah wouldna bruit that opinion aboot, if Ah were you.'

'But you're not me,' I wanted to say. Somehow the turn this dialogue had taken had suddenly – and rather unreasonably - got under my skin. Instead I confined myself to responding that I had no intention of remaining in the Service, that I had a marriage planned for the spring, by which time I would be elsewhere.

'Ye may find it's nae as easy as ye think, Jamie,' Gordon remarked.

I shrugged. 'Maybe not.' Then I thought I should kick the conversation into a more gossipy furrow. 'I guessed from his age that Mr Pennington probably had a past…'

'Och, he's got that all reet,' said Gordon drily, breaking in with a short laugh.

I waited for more, but nothing happened, so I attempted a prompt. 'Bearing in mind his age,' I ventured, 'I supposed he had served under Captain Brownhall during the war.'

Gordon cocked an eye at me. 'Nae, lad, naething o' the kind…quite the contrary in fact.'

To prevent me learning any more, it seemed, Gordon rose to

his feet and drew the Night Order Book from its nook in the book-shelf. He wrote what he had written countless nights before, signed them and asked me to counter-sign before biding me good-night and disappearing below.

Having twiddled with the oscilloscope of the LORAN I plotted the ship's position, updated the Comms. Office and went out through the black-out curtain into the pitch darkness of the wheel-house.

'Go on laddie,' I heard McGrigor prompt Hamish and awaited the report.

'Naething in sicht…' Hamish's voice was full of teen-age resentment.

'Sir,' McGrigor said in the gloom.

'Sir,' complied Hamish after a short hesitation.

'Nothing in sight,' I responded. There rarely was but I disliked Hamish's tone of voice. However, I added 'Thank you,' as I would have if McGrigor had made the report – which of course he had in effect.

Despite the red lighting of the chart-room it took me a moment to acquire night-vision, but even without it, I could see the breaking wave-crests to windward as the bloody ship rolled and rolled.

*

It was difficult to do it at night, when the Able-seaman and Deck-boy kept one company inside the wheel-house without their other small tasks to attend to, but the trick with the rolling was to pace the wheel-house on the down-hill roll. That way one did not exhaust oneself, but kept awake and alert and was ready to move to check the radar, put the ship's position on the station chart – a large scale Perspex covered document on which we wrote with china-graph pencils.

Otherwise one could also jam oneself into a nook or cranny, especially at the navigational radar, but this could induce a soporific effect, a thing to be avoided at all costs. Such jamming-in, was impossible at the chart-table. Here one had to position oneself with legs wide-splayed, leaning over the chart, the log-book or one's sight-book if one had just taken a sun or star observation. Since this required the consultation of the Nautical Almanac, containing the day's ephemeris, and a copy of Nautical Tables such as the Norie's version I favoured, keeping all these bits and bobs from sliding off onto the deck was not so much a challenge as tiresome, irritatingly, temper-inducingly tiresome. And although we had only been at sea for a few days, we were already short of proper sleep, something we would only get once back in port, or, if we were really fortunate, if the wind and the eternal bloody swell died down – which it never did even in periods of dead calm.

As a small compensation, and when we had the bridge to our own, I put on the small Eddystone radio receiver in the chart-room and tuned in to Radio Luxemburg. I recall *Matthew & Son* sung by Cat Stevens – as he was then known – being played a good deal, along with The Monkeys' *Last Train to Clarksville*. Anything by The Beatles or the Rolling Stones, and I increased the volume. I don't think McGrigor approved of this, but I caught Hamish humming and tapping out a rhythm or two.

To some extent pop music blunted one's sensibilities, though it also reminded one of what one was missing ashore. And it if it did not prevent one from thinking about girls and dances and such-like, it did divert you from more introspective broodings. In the aftermath of my conversation with Captain Gordon I had quite forgotten to query why Mackenzie had lied to me, though perhaps lie was too strong a word. But I was even more intrigued by the person of Charles, never ever call me Charlie, Pennington.

That first Saturday night out we enjoyed our traditional 'party' in the Chief Steward's cabin. Most of the participants were day-worker who didn't keep a watch: Ted Wilkins and his boss, the Senior Met. Officer, Bill Collins, another Sassenach; the Senior Radar and the Electrical Officers, along with Colin Buchanan and myself who joined after midnight. We were all jammed in higgledy-piggledy, several of us on the Chief Steward's bunk, his day-bed, or settee, with the man himself, Chris Gilshaw, lolling in desk chair. Late comers had to sit on the deck, or Chris's upturned rosy – a can for his waste paper, fag-ends and so forth. Most of us smoked and the air grew thick with the noxious fumes of duty-free fags and a free-ranging conversation that I cannot possibly reproduce but would have surprised any eaves-dropper, for we were not averse to tackling any subject, all of which was accompanied by a modest binging of our hoarded allowance of beer and spirits.

Since these informal gatherings were passed like miles-stones one tended to remember their occurrence rather better than their content and the importance of this one in terms of recollection was two-fold. The first reason I recall it was that I didn't ask around to see if anyone else knew anything about Pennington. I felt it would not go down well, would mark me out as nosy and somehow prejudice the little niche I had made for myself in the company of my fellow revellers. But I was pretty certain that Bill Collins, or the Senior Radar Officer, an ex-RAF warrant officer improbably named Jasper Cordwainer, both of whom had been in the *Guardian* for some time, would have a good idea of Pennington's back-story. As for Dougal Henty, although he had referred to Pennington as 'oor Charlie' and to something about a uterine passage, well he was a closed book; apart from our passing in the ward-room at mealtimes, I saw little of him.

However, I had better access to his fellow joker, Iain Mackenzie, though the First Officer rarely hung about after I had relieved him and seemed not inclined to gossip unless with Henty or another of the ship's more senior officers than myself.

The second reason I recall that first Saturday was that by the time turned-in at 02.30, the ship was rolling a good deal less. Moreover, the following forenoon proved to be almost lovely, for the wind had dropped to a gentle breeze and the swells could be seen rolling down on us like huge, smooth hilly ridges, great parallel wave-forms, with the air miraculously full of bird life, gannets, the ubiquitous fulmars and the pretty kittiwakes, both handsomely dove-grey in their maturity and with the strongly black barred wings of their immature off-spring.

The sun has risen redly through a thin grey layer of high cloud which, during the day, slowly cleared away. But if the red-sky at dawning was the shepherd's warning, it proved to be a false rumour on Ocean Station INDIA that day. Although the sky was never a radiant blue

It became a hard, pale and cold blue, the light wind slowly veering into the north-west.

Pennington relieved me at 12.30 with one of his by-now customary one liner portentous remarks: 'Something's in the air, Jamie…' which was pretty right-on for a bloke sitting aboard a weather ship observing meteorological phenomena for the benefit of an unknowing public several hundred miles to the east-south-east!

The weather held all that Sunday. There was a film show that evening in the Petty-Officer's mess. With timings being staggered for the watch-keepers, I missed this, though I had seen its predecessor, the old Western classic *Bad Day at Black Rock*, starring Spencer Tracy, which I had watched with Ted Wilkins. That evening it was *Fantastic Voyage* starring, of all people, the voluptuous Raquel Welch.

Licking his lips with exaggerated but salacious anticipation Mackenzie scuttled off to watch it. By way of compensation, shortly after I had taken over from him, as the twilight deepened, I got a first-class five-star fix, which put us right on our LORAN position. I also took the opportunity of taking an azimuth to verify the accuracy of our gyro compass and by 21.00 was feeling pretty chipper with myself, stowing away my sextant and books when the inter-com came through: 'Met. to Bridge.' I recognised Ted's voice.

I was already aware that the light breeze and the colder air had extended the balloon ascent and was expecting some comment on this, for Ted knew that I kept a daily Journal and took an interest in what was going on elsewhere in the ship.

'Bridge, Met.,' I responded.

'Have you taken a look outside in the last quarter of an hour, Jamie?' Ted asked.

A sudden sense of alarm flooded me. I had regularly checked the surface scanning navigational radar whilst working out my sights, but I dropped the intercom and rushed out into the wheel-house where McGrigor stood smoking by the forward wheel-house windows, his rugged face lit by the fag-ends and reflected in the armoured glass.

'Ah've sent the lad doon below, sir, tae get ma tobaccy…'

I ignored McGrigor, terrified that a ship was bearing down upon us from astern - why else would Ted be reporting it if not from that direction? Our navigational radar had blind arcs astern, something one had to bear in mind… Anyway, thinking we were about to be run down I threw open the wheel-house door and stared aft, over the jumble of superstructures and past the mainmast and the higher obstructions of the Bofors guns and the hangar.

I had had such a shock that it took me a moment to realise that far from a ship's navigation lights bearing down upon us, everything was oddly lit-up by a strange pulsing lambency.

It was only then that I looked up into the sky and saw it, the *Aurora Borealis*.

*

As it happened I could scarcely be blamed for not seeing it sooner. Being down aft and out on deck checking the hydrogen bottles were all secure for the night before he knocked off after the prolonged balloon flight, Ted had spotted the auroral display in its infancy. Indeed, by the time I was staring up at it, although already impressive, it was some way off attaining the majesty it would assume before it would eventually fade away. But by 22.30, by which time Ted had joined me on the bridge, it was, I think, the most impressive natural phenomenon I had ever seen. I think I can say that even after all these years, when I have seen it several times, that display in December 1966 was outstanding.

It matured into a fantastical manifestation of one of the great mysteries of the earth, with vast pulsating curtains of cold green fire that seemed to hang down from what appeared to be a height far greater than that of the stars. These rippled, as though blown by a cosmic wind, while enormous rays stretched upwards to the zenith. It was unbelievably beautiful, and somewhat terrifying in its magnificent extent, which seemed to hint at the infinitude of space and of the utter and incomprehensible vastness of the cosmos. We stood spell-bound, our eyes upwards, impervious to the cold, the hairs on the back of our necks crawling with the numinous quality of the experience.

After about twenty minutes I telephoned the Old Man's cabin to inform him; predictably he thanked me before telling me that he had 'seen it before'. Which was undoubtedly true but I felt he was missing out. Still that left it to Ted and me, and McGrigor and Hamish who stood looking aloft like us with his mouth open. 'Fucking hell,' I heard the boy breathe in awe. I have no doubt that upon occasion the aurora could be seen from Glasgow, but the city's lights and the lad's lack of schooling in such matters had presumably denied him the experience of observing it before. But the sheer splendour of that night's display would have stopped the mouth of even the most blasé observer. And indeed it did. After about a quarter of an hour Captain Gordon appeared on the bridge and joined us. Soon afterwards the Chief Engineer arrived, along with others and although they did not linger long in the cold, their hushed whispers made me think that we were in the presence of Almighty God – or something very like Him.

After a while most of our companions drifted away. Some such display was not unusual hereabouts, though there was mention of more active and colourful spectacles having been seen from O.S. ALPHA in the Denmark Strait.

As midnight approached my 'guests' on the bridge, including Captain Gordon had all retreated into the warmth of the ship and the comfort of their bunks. McGrigor had returned to smoking in his usual post when not steering and Hamish had decided that picking his nose would yield more satisfaction than standing next to the Sassenach Third Officer whom he had – reluctantly - to address as 'sir'.

With ten or so minutes to go I read the barometer, the thermometer and the windward anemometer and wrote up the deck log for the watch. I signed this then took another look outside. The aurora blazed as splendidly as ever and I stood there, thinking that if I left the Service sooner rather than later, I might never see anything like it again. And that is where I was when Charles Pennington appeared on the bridge to relieve me.

*

I heard him coming, of course. Even on the bridge wing his voice carried to me, though I forget exactly what he was singing, so wrapt was I in the experience of the aurora. In fact my over-riding thought was that he should shut-up, that the magic of the night was totally ruined by the intrusion.

But he stopped as he stepped out onto the bridge wing, remarking with a sudden awe, 'On such a night as this, under the Alexandrine sky, did great Ptolemy stand to cast his eye, aloft upon the glitt'ring and encircling stars, and therein grasped the reason *why...*' His voice trailed off, introspectively.

'Who wrote that?' I asked, a tad embarrassed by this versifying.

'Pennington, dear boy, 'tis pure Pennington,' he answered almost abstractedly, before adding, with an almost reverential wonder, 'Oh, Jamie, look at it...just look at it...'

'I have been,' I retorted.

'Has it been going on long?' he asked.

'About three hours.'

'You lucky sod... God but it's magnificent...magnificent...one of the best displays that I have seen...'

'I'm told they are better up on ALPHA,' I said.

He paused, then added, his voice almost conspiratorially low, as if imparting some great secret, or words of wisdom: 'yes, perhaps in some ways,' he paused again, as if unwilling to say more, before going on: 'and I've seen some superb manifestations in the Barents Sea, but this is no less tremendous. Fix it in your head, Jamie; one day you'll take great comfort from the memory.'

We both stood there until I gave an enormous and involuntary shiver. It was not from the effects of the aurora, wondrous though they were: I had become bitterly cold.

'Get yourself inside, laddie, before you freeze to death,' Pennington commanded.

I hadn't realised how chilled I had become and was about to go below before I realised that my hands were too cold to use the vertical ladder rungs. Pennington saw my problem and ordered me into the chart-room and poured me a mug of hot tea.

'We don't know enough about this lot,' he said jerking his head as though at the sky, while I stood shivering and thawing out close to the chart-room radiator. 'You know, Jamie, it's always puzzled me why we call what we are out here to support *meteorology*. It's got nothing to do with meteors, for heaven's sake. Our eighteenth century forbears called it *atmosphereolgy*, a much more appropriate term to my mind.'

My teeth were chattering now as Pennington went on. 'Still, there we are, greater minds and all that, but notwithstanding the effects of solar winds changing the trajectories of charged particles in the magnetosphere and in ionising them producing light, blah, blah, blah, we are all part of this you know.'

'We are?' I said, only half paying attention as I warmed up and thought myself a bloody fool for getting so cold.

'Oh, indeed we are,' Pennington went on, easing himself down on the chart-room settee and almost transfixing me with his darkly glittering eyes. Thinking back, he was a weird spectacle, half lit by the red light that illuminated the space. Somehow he held my attention like Taylor Coleridge's Ancient Mariner had pinned that of the wedding guest.

'That marvel,' he said, gesturing outside through the chart-room windows, 'involves the earth's magnetic field, itself a wondrous thing when you think of it. Imagine those old seafarers discovering the magic of the lodestone. They could venture in a given direction, the wind being in their favour… There it was, the lodestone, lying about for man to pick-up and profit by when the time was right… D'you follow me, Jamie?'

'Yes,' I said cautiously.

'And then there's this ship. She begins her life lying on a builder's slipway, a few plates and girders at first, then frames and all the rest of it are added. Gradually she takes up a molecular structure dependent upon her physical attitude to the earth's magnetic field, a fact which used to bedevil the use of magnetic compasses before deviation was thoroughly understood. But you know all this…'

I was not sure where all this was going. It was almost 01.00

and I was ready for my bunk. Nevertheless, I made some sound of assent.

'And then there is us, Jamie, us…you and me. We too are possessed of two great attributes that are generally over-looked. The first is what the Quakers call the light within us; the second, of which I am reminded tonight, is our inherent and personal magnetism. Now, I'm not talking about charisma or charm, but the physical alignment of our individual corporeal molecules. This, like the ship's permanent magnetism, stays with us all our lives. D'you know how we acquire this state of fixed magnetic charge? No, of course you don't, but we get it during our birth. The old astrologers thought it was all something to do with the alignment of planets and so forth, but they only grasped half the story. A moment's reflection would have told then that this was crap. At any given moment, countless children are born; but that same countless number of children do not enjoy or suffer the same outcomes in their lives, or later die at the same moment.

'No, the old astro-boys were barking up the wrong tree; the secret lies instead in our emergence upon the world's stage down the uterine passage, we are disinvaginated by our mothers and therein lies our luck, our fortune…'

I have no idea what sort of expression was on my face, but I recalled the in-joke between Mackenzie and Henty. Was Pennington utterly mad? That he was odd, was certain; that he had a past, was equally so; nor was he the first person I had encountered at sea with a rather idiosyncratic view of the human condition and a penchant for airing it. Gazing at the wonders of the deep, and especially the firmament, from a ship's bridge was – and I suppose still is – liable to focus a questioning intellect. And remember, although Crick and Watson had gained the Nobel prize for their work on DNA in 1962, the implications of their discoveries and what flowed from them were not well known even four years later, and certainly not among Britain's still then considerable seafaring population. What *was* curious though, was that during the Second World War Francis Crick worked for the Admiralty, developing magnetic mines – a fact that I only discovered later. Looking back, I have often thought it something of a coincidence.

Anyway, there Pennington sat, looking half-demonic under the red lighting with his great grey beard and lined cheeks, spouting his theory about the uterine passage and personal magnetism, while I – now more or less back to my natural temperature – stood with my back against the chart-table, legs splayed, wondering quite how to process it all.

But it seemed that Pennington too had come to the end of his peroration. 'So there you are Jamie: magnetism. It makes us who we are, sets us up for life…' his voice trailed off, then rallied as he stood up and stretched. 'Or otherwise, Jamie, or otherwise…' His voice took on a wistful quality and I blurted out:

'You mean it can set one on a downward trajectory as well as an upward one?'

I cannot explain how I knew, perhaps I only did so much later, when I finally understood the fellow, but despite the concealing nature of the grey beard and the half-light, he turned away as though I had slapped his face.

'Time for bed,' he said sharply, ignoring my query and passing out of the chart-room into the wheelhouse, still faintly lit by the green auroral light. I followed, but did not linger. With a general 'good-night,' I scrambled below to the welcome warmth of my bunk.

3

I was fortunate that I did not catch a cold from my exposure and if I did not immediately forget the curious monologue Pennington had delivered, it soon faded in my memory as the activities of our daily toil overtook us all. The constant routine, the rolling and the tiredness drove lateral thoughts out of one's head; it took a good deal of intellectual rigour to accomplish one's daily duty.

And so, after the previous night's somewhat surreal quality, the following morning proved more typical with a south-westerly Force 9 strong gale blowing. Despite this, orders were passed to take deep-specimens of sea-water samples.

You may recollect my mentioning the special winch-housing on the old gun-platform with its immensely long wire. To take samples we called out a special party, with Mackenzie taking charge of the winch-party. The winch wire was run out of the deck-house, through a special davit and, with a heavy weight on it, slowly lowered into the sea. At intervals prescribed by our special orders, a Nansen bottle was fitted. Each of these – invented by the famous Norwegian polar explorer – had a small lead weight suspended underneath it. When the wire had been lowered down to a depth of 2,000 metres, another lead weight was clamped loosely round the wire and let go. It disappeared into the water and struck the top of the first Nansen bottle it encountered. This tripped the bottle, which turned over and captured a sample of sea-water at the depth at which it was set, simultaneously releasing the lead weight beneath it. This descended to the next bottle, setting off a chain-reaction until the last bottle was operated, at which time we began the long upward haul, carefully removing each bottle, noting the depth and placing it in the crates provided. On our return to Greenock these would be carted away to scientific analysis. We carried out these deep-sounding operations several times in the voyage and they were, I was told, intended to provide information about salinity and hence density levels for, *inter alia*, submarine operations in the North Atlantic.

The work was long and chillingly cold, especially for the seamen handling the Nansen bottles at the ship's side, but to facilitate the operation, despite the wind-speed and sea-state, the ship was hove-to. However, this was not accomplished in the conventional sense by manoeuvring the ship head to wind, but putting the engines slow astern, so that she cocked her stern up into the wind.

Although Captain Gordon appeared on the bridge for all this, which occurred in my watch, he simply told me to 'carry on' and let me get on with it. Putting the engines slow-astern drew her round, seeking the wind's eye, but even at the minimum revs necessary to hold her with the gale on the port quarter, the *Weather Guardian*'s square transom stern met the on-coming breaking seas with the resistance of a brick wall. The whole ship shuddered with the impact every few minutes for the two hours it took to complete the task, for the weather was ferocious. The ground swells were up to forty feet in height with sea-waves of ten feet 'on top'. How the old girl stood it, I know not, for she would ship a green sea which filled her whole after deck as high as the bulwark, roaring and sloshing about the open hangar as if it was a cave. On my first voyage I had asked the Old Man why we carried out this task in such atrocious weather, to which he replied curtly: 'Orders,' which led me to suppose the time and date were somehow important to those who manipulated us. Thus, to Captain Gordon and the rest of us, it became all part of a day's work and I felt pretty chipper at playing my part in it, very grateful for the Old Man's obvious faith in me.

Pennington took no formal part in the evolution, he was watch-below anyway, but as from the bridge wing I kept an eye astern, I saw him, standing on the Bofors gun-platform. I thought at first he was taking photographs, because it was all pretty impressive, but then I realised – with a bit of a shock – that he was enacting something by himself. That's the only way I can put it. The Old Man came out of the wheel-house at one point and stood next to me, watching him.

'He'll be alright,' Gordon muttered to me. 'He does this occasionally; he's enjoying himself.'

The Captain seemed to be correct. During our deep-soundings, the wind had been increasing and two hours after we had finished, towards noon, it was blowing harder than ever and had backed a couple of points. We were now in excess of 20 miles to leeward of *Oscar Sierra* and, picking my moment, I turned the ship back into the wind. This was always a dangerous and tricky manoeuvre, requiring a cool head and fine judgement; it was also exciting, and one craved that!

We carried out the noon balloon ascent and began the slow, very slow, business of working our way 20 miles up-wind of our On Station position. At 12.30 a very cheerful Pennington came up to relieve me, threw open both wheel-house doors and went out to literally sniff the wind, raising his nose like a bloody pointer.

The west-south-westerly wind had now reached Storm Force 10, with the windward anemometer showing gusts of Force 13 (73 knots and way over hurricane force at 65). In the gusts the needle of the aneroid barometer we had in the chart-room would 'twitch' from the compression of the air in the enclosed bridge.

Such a magnitude of air movement generated big waves over a huge swell, a prospect of white streaks of spume and 'smoke,' the latter caused by the wind lifting the sea's surface and atomising it, sending it to leeward like bird-shot. Outside, on any exposed deck. it was actually quite difficult to breathe.

In such heavy conditions, individual wave crests could be as much as half a mile apart while the wave height from trough to crest could range up to fifty feet and more. In the trough the ship often experienced little wind, for most of it passed over her, but as she climbed the face of the advancing swell, surmounted as it is by the wind-generated sea-wave, this increased. The wind-noise gradually grew to a crescendo, a demonic scream in a strong gale, and in storm conditions a booming – described by our predecessors as 'blowing great guns' as it played through the lattice mast, the rigging and antennae. It is amid the turbulence of a heavy breaking sea that damage may be done. In such conditions the officer-of-the-watch had to con the ship, wave by wave, ordering the helmsman to alter course to meet each breaking wave and minimise damage as we lay hove-to, steaming slowly ahead and adjusting engine revolutions to meet the constantly changing situation.

Handing over, I left Pennington to it, heading for an uncomfortable dinner and an afternoon in my bunk. I don't know how long Pennington stood out on the bridge wing. It was surrounded by steel baffles that threw the passing air upwards, but he was obviously once again enjoying himself.

The following days were full of this sort of thing, though with intermittent breaks. We took more deep-sea samples and I continued to take my plankton hauls. We engaged in other scientific activities, like trailing a bathythermograph, while the Met-Boys regularly flew off their radio-sondes at some risk to life and limb, collected surface sea-water temperatures, obtained salinity samples and checked our various arrays which collected other data such as the amount and intensity of something called sunlight, which seemed as rare as hen's teeth. I would occasionally visit Ted in the Met. Office where an impressive collection of what he called 'boxes of tricks' - early computers - did their thing. He and his team laid out synoptic charts with the skill and keen eyes of dedicated draughtsman, a real achievement given the constant movement of the ship which put the petty frustrations of trying to eat a meal at a table partitioned off by wooden fiddles into its proper perspective!

About the only event of note occurred one evening when I had sent McGrigor off on some errand. The weather was moderate and I was giving Hamish a long trick at the wheel as we repositioned the ship. He had had some hours of schooling in steering and been hold how to respond properly to my orders and was shaping-up rather well with old McGrigor as his sea-daddy.

I was walking up and down the wheelhouse when, out of the blue, Hamish asked: 'Why dae Ah ha'e to call ye, "sir".'

I stopped in front of the telemotor so that there was some illumination on my face and I explained.

'Because, Hamish, 'I'm an officer, and specifically because I'm officer-of-the-watch and normally in charge of the ship for eight hours out of twenty four. Moreover, I've got qualifications to prove my experience and knowledge, and because a ship cannot function properly without a degree of discipline and respect…'

'So it's nae because ye're English?'

'No,' I responded, taken aback. 'Did you think it was?' I saw him shrug. 'You call Mr Mackenzie "sir," don't you? And Captain Gordon and Mr Pennington.'

'Aye, but they're older than yersel'.'

I couldn't think of anything to say to this to promote my damaged ego, then something occurred to me. 'Look Hamish, I can see why it might irk you a bit to have to call me "sir," but you've seen me taking sights with my sextant, haven't you, eh?'

'Aye.'

'Well, there's actually nothing stopping you from learning how to do all the things that I can do, of sitting for your Second Mate's Certificate of Competence and one day filling my boots. One day you could be a Master Mariner like Captain Gordon or Mr Mackenzie…it wouldn't be unusual for a lad like you.' Hamish grunted, with what reaction I could not say, so I added for good measure: 'Of course, you'd have to work hard, but usually lads like you find someone to help them.'

It was an interesting little conversation because it reminded me that perhaps the only truly meritocratic institution the British ever produced outside a time of war when the usual barriers were swept away, was the Merchant Navy. I explained that he would have to join a regular merchant ship, and leave his ma's apron strings, but he'd get to see something of the world and countless sons of Glasgow, like those from Newcastle, Liverpool and elsewhere, had found their metier at sea, or used the experience as stepping stones to something better than an uncertain life of impoverishment.

At the time I thought it all went down like a lead balloon.

*

A few nights later, after an exhausting evening watch of constantly conning the ship through heavy seas, meeting each grey-beard as it loomed at us through the darkness, the ship shuddering at the impact as her bow clove the breaker and the howl of each successive gale lingered long after one had come below, I turned-in dog tired. As usual, after a few minutes reading, I went to sleep quite quickly; it was staying asleep that was difficult. I had already been thrown out of my bunk twice that trip, but that particular night, at about 04.30 I was woken by sea-water pouring out of the deck-head lining above my head.

This was something I had never experienced before and I was alarmed. I shot out of my bunk, dragging on some clothes and made my way up to the bridge. I had thought the entire ship would have been aroused, but that was not so and I never discovered why no-one else along the port alleyway had suffered the deluge. Perhaps it was some trick of the ventilation trunking, but there was water aplenty in the wheel-house, pouring down the access hatch as if we were a submarine. I dragged myself up and found Iain Mackenzie sloshing about in some six inches of the North Atlantic. In the light of the binnacle I could see the grin on the face of his helmsman as he asked, 'Canna ye sleep, Jamie?'

'What the fuck happened?' I countered with a deep irritation, 'I've had half the fucking Western Ocean deposited on my fucking bunk!'

'Och, we took a big one. Come away into the chart-room, Ah've just put the kettle on.'

Five minutes later I was ensconced on the chart-room settee with Iain standing by the chart-table – the reverse of my position *vis-à-vis* Pennington on the night of the aurora. For a moment neither of us said a word, then Mackenzie remarked with a chuckle, 'Ah'm surprised we didna put oot the boiler! Dougal's just phoned me. I think he thought we'd all been swept off the upper deck, bridge an a'.'

'What did she do? Roll on a downward pitch?'

'Ah hav'na the foggiest idea. Ye'd better ask ma airse, since it was uppermost. I was flung across the bluidy wheelhouse. Only Corrigan kept his footing and he had the helm and telemotor tae cling to!'

'Bloody hell.'

We sipped our tea as the *Guardian* continued to bang and shudder her weary way to windward at less than half a knot.

Mackenzie did not apparently feel the need to con her through each wave as I had been taught to on my first voyage in the ship. Perhaps that was why had had got flung arse-uppermost, but the circumstance now paid a surprising dividend.

Mackenzie offered me a cigarette. I was a light smoker, consuming five or six a day, but no more. Anyway, I accepted the offer and the light that came with it. I didn't feel tired anymore and the prospect of returning to a wet bed had no appeal. I knew I could dry the damned thing out later by hanging it in the upper parts of the forward boiler-room, but not at that hour of the morning.

Mackenzie was glad of the company, I think, for he said, 'Ah'm surprised Pennington isna oop here.'

To which I responded, 'well he didn't get washed out of his bloody bunk.'

'No, but he loves this sort of thing…'

'Christ knows why,' I remarked, and then I said something stupid. 'D'you think he's mad?'

Mackenzie looked at me and shook his head. 'You shouldna'…'

'No, I'm sorry,' I apologised quickly, 'I shouldn't have asked that…'

'He's nae mad, Jamie,' Mackenzie said quietly, 'but he's troubled.'

'I'm sorry,' I repeated, thoroughly chastened. 'I gathered that…' and then I rallied, recalling the conversation and the big fib Iain Mackezie had told me back in Greenock. 'I just wondered,' I blundered on. 'He spoke to me the other night about his magnetic theory and the uterine passage…'

'Och, that nonsense,' chuckled Mackenzie. 'Ah see what makes ye think he's no' all there.'

'And to be fair, Iain,' I added, now emboldened, 'you did misinform me when you said he'd been called from the *Weather*

Follower. The Old Man put me right on that score. I know that he has some connection with Captain Brownhall.'

'It goes back a long way, Jamie. I dinna really know the full story mysel', but it's got something tae do with the last war. Charlie Pennington was decorated Ah, believe, but its nae my business an' it best if you dinna make it yours. D'ye ken ma meaning?'

I nodded. 'Yes, of course.' I felt mortified alright, almost told-off like a naughty school-boy.

'He's an efficient officer,' Mackenzie went on, his voice kinder, mollifying, 'an intelligent an' well educated man. He doesna' drink and he doesna' smoke much, so we can leave him his wee eccentricities…'

'Such as the uterine passage?' I remarked, in an attempt to further lighten the mood and claw back some regard from the First Officer. I had no desire whatsoever for Iain Mackenzie to think ill of me, nor of word of my intemperate remark to reach the ears of Charles Pennington.

*

Christmas was now approaching and our thoughts inevitably dwelt upon what we were going to miss. We had been furnished with a 'last date' for posting anything to us for Christmas. Letters and cards, of course, but gifts had to be small and light, token really, something like a tube of Smarties or a Mars Bar. I think that it was during the early forenoon of the 22nd December when at about 08.40 we received a signal from an airborne RAF Shackleton from Kinloss, Morayshire. Although she informed us that she bore our Christmas mail, there was no prior warning because the aircraft's sortie was ostensibly to carry out an air-sea rescue exercise with us. She would, she added, be accompanied by a second Shackleton from Ballykelly, Northern Ireland, which was to take photographs.

It was blowing from the west-south-west, Force 6/7 with a

fine drizzle and very poor visibility and once made aware of the evolution, the deck-hands were ordered to stations for 'a ditching exercise'. This was intended to test our ability to provide a flare-path for a civil air-liner compelled to ditch in the North Atlantic. The idea was that we vectored the disabled aircraft onto the flare path and were waiting at its terminal point, ready to render assistance with a rescue boat turned out in the davits. It was a plan that struck most of us as wildly optimistic, though we had details of the weak-points in the fuselages of all commercial air-liners then working the North Atlantic through which we were directed to break-in to rescue the passengers.

The Radar Office had just finished tracking the 06.00 balloon flight as the deck department assembled at their various posts. Captain Gordon relieved me and took over the con and poor old Pennington, having been turned out of his bunk early, was instructed to work out the best option – given the wind direction and sea-state – to lay a flare-path. Mackenzie took charge of the upper deck with the Bosun and a number of Able-seamen, ready to both recover our mail and – if only in simulation – provide a launching party for the leeward motor-boat which was in my charge. Besides four seamen and the three deck-boys, Colin Buchanan and an engine-room greaser were on hand to run the boat's engine and provide extra man-power.

I won't bore you with Pennington's task but the idea was for the ship to steam along the most favourable line, relative to the rolling seas and swells, to provide the smoothest path for an aircraft to ditch. Mackenzie's deck-party chucked flares over the side at intervals when the order came from the bridge, while the ship, steaming at full speed, then stopped near the last flare, ready to launch my boat and go to the rescue.

By the time we were approaching the distal-point of our flare-path, which lay roughly north-north-west to south-south-east, our tracking radar was feeding the Shackletons' approaching positions to the bridge from where Pennington, talking to them via the medium frequency radio-telephone - skilfully vectored them over the first flare, laid at the northerly end of the flare path, 10 miles away. The engine-room was now ordered to 'make smoke!' and a filthy black cloud blossomed from our funnel and streamed away to leeward. Well, most of it did; some of it was caught in eddies and down-draughts round the superstructure and set all of us sitting in the boat into a fit of coughing.

The aircraft were not flying very high and the first soon reported visual sightings of the first of our flares, turned onto the bearing of the flare-path on Pennington's advice, and dropped to a low altitude. As yet we could not yet see them in the lousy visibility and the first intimation of their proximity was the noise of their engines, four Rolls Royce Griffons to each of them.

Shackleton *MZF*, which was masquerading as the disabled air-liner, broke cloud cover at 200 feet, less than 2 miles from us. *MZF* passed us at 150 feet with a great roar, simulating a ditching alongside us, thus completing the formal exercise with a mutual exchange of bridge-to-flight-deck remarks.

This did not complete the morning's fun, however, for *MZF* circled us and was joined by her consort until they had jockeyed into position while Captain Gordon turned the *Weather Guardian* head to sea.

The two big aircraft then came roaring in along our starboard side, the second Shackleton flying *en echelon* at a slightly higher altitude. There was much cordial waving between our bridge and their cockpits before they turned to make their final run, the mail-drop. Back they came, *MZF* with her bomb-doors agape, a huge dark bird, little higher than our mastheads – and a mere 90 to 100 feet laterally from the ship. Two small yellow canisters were dropped into the sea on small parachutes, whereupon both Shackletons swung away to the eastwards, climbed out of sight into the murk and were gone.

As the aircraft droned away far above the low scud the Old Man let the ship drift down on the brightly coloured containers which were picked up with by the Bosun using a grapnel on a light line.

After this excitement, routine took over again. I returned to the bridge to complete the watch. Below someone, I forget who, sorted the mail. At dinner someone else, Jasper Cordwainer if I remember correctly, added to the comments about that morning's exercise by reminding us all that the Pathé newsreels that accompanied most feature films would probably show a short clip of a lonely Ocean Weather Ship in the North Atlantic. The commentator would doubtless tell the cinema audience that she was full of plucky Brits collecting data so that Bracknell's ace-forecasters could predict whether the nation was to have a white Christmas.

'Either that,' someone else contributed, 'or else it will be some bloody boat going out to a lighthouse…'

I left my mail for Christmas Day. Delayed gratification was not a principle of mine, but Christmas would be pretty flat without something to open. I did, however, note that my widowed mother had sent me a small parcel and a card, and Sukie, my fiancée, what looked like – and I hoped was - a love-letter, as well as a small package. I tucked these all away safely, a bit choked with unexpected emotion.

That afternoon, following the distribution of mail throughout the ship, a number of us decorated the ward-room for Christmas. We had some paper-chains and some tinsel, dug out of the Chief Steward's store. The Old Man would give a prize for the best decorated mess-room and it was 'not done' for the officers to win. The palm usually went to the Ratings' Mess, though the long-serving Petty-Officers usually actually made the best showing.

Preparations for the big day were now well under way, but on the morning of the 23rd we carried out the second part of our air/sea rescue drill. Captain Gordon took advantage of a beautiful morning. With barely a breath of wind, under a blue sky and with only a low ground swell to trouble us, we lowered one of the ship's motor lifeboats which I took away from the ship's side. Of course, the conditions were as ideal as one could possibly wish for in the North Atlantic and we all knew that should we ever have to go to the aid of another ship or a ditched aircraft of any type, circumstances were likely to be very different.

Nevertheless, it was a good opportunity for practice and there was no point in carrying out such an evolution in conditions where someone could be injured, or gear smashed such that – should the fan and faeces collide for real – our capability was reduced. We had some heavy human dummies to throw into the sea and then haul out again, and we stopped the boat's engine and got the oars out for a bit. Had there been any wind, we would have rigged the boat's mast and set sail for what was laughably termed a 'yachting' trip, but that would have been completely futile.

Nevertheless, from two miles away and despite her orange upper-works, the ship was not only uniformly grey against a rose-red sunrise, but looked insubstantial. I reflected on the depth below us; it was a bloody long way. I thought too, of the wrecks that littered it, the ships, men and *matériel* sent to the bottom in the Battle of Atlantic. This, the longest battle of the Second World War, had cast its shadow over my own life, for my father – the Chief Mate of a merchantman - had been lost somewhere out here, when his ship had been torpedoed.

As an early twilight closed over us that evening it brought with us a mist and in the mist a surface radar-echo. I had just come on watch and was monitoring the approaching vessel, the first we had seen since our leave-taking from the *Stratus*. We did not actually see her until she was about three miles away. Unsurprisingly she turned out to be a Soviet spy-ship, a trawler-type vessel but bristling with more aerials and antennae than a porcupine had quills.

She passed us about half a mile away, the thump-thump of her diesels coming to us over the still calm sea. She gave us a blast on her siren by way of an acknowledgement of her passing. Almost as soon as this intruder had vanished, and in quick succession we received two alerts. A Panamanian tramp-ship declared an unspecified distress, then inexplicably cancelled it. Like London buses, after days of nothing but routine, forty minutes later a second potential emergency was patched through from the Radio Control Room. Comms informed us that a Dutch air-liner had turned back towards Europe with engine trouble; we had monitored some of this traffic on the bridge, but apart from raising our state of readiness for about half an hour, nothing further transpired until, at about 23.40 I went to write up the deck-log for midnight.

I took a look at the aneroid barometer, I remember, and was actually in the very act of verifying its reading with reference to the barograph, when the intercom burst into life.

'Met. to Bridge…' I thought it was the usual preparatory warning that the Met. Assistants were about to go on deck to fill the midnight balloon.

'Bridge to Met. Go ahead,' I said, deferring my task of comparing the aneroid barometer with the barometer's ink tracing for a moment or two.

'We're filling the balloon now.'

'Roger that,' I said, ready to hang up.

'Radar to Bridge and Met, copied that…' Cordwainer's boys were on the ball. 'All ready here.'

'Met to Bridge, that's not all…'

'Bridge, Met., go ahead.'

'We've got a very steep drop in air pressure down here. It's fallen off a cliff in the last few minutes.'

'Is that you Ted?' I asked.

'Yes, Jamie.'

'I'd just noticed that myself.' I looked at the anemometer readings which were repeated both in the chart-room and down aft in the Met. Office. We always consulted the windward one, and as the ship was stationary, there was no ship's wind to confuse the reading. 'I've only got four to five knots of wind here…'

'Yup, but it's been backing…' Ted said. I checked the direction; he was right.

'Hang on a moment.'

I went out into the wheel-house. McGrigor was at the forward window, a roll-up glowing in his mouth. Hamish had been sent below to wash the mugs and tea-spoons and top-up our sealed milk container.

I flung back the port wheel-house door and stepped out onto the bridge-wing. It was noticeably warmer than when I had watched the Russian spy-trawler pass earlier. I took a good look round, scanning the horizon, a kind of prickling in the hairs at the nape of my neck. The calm and lovely quiet of that early morning run in the motor lifeboat had turned into an ominous kind of foreboding. I looked up; not a star was to be seen and I could not even guess at what altitude the overcast lay. At that moment it seemed decidedly odd that I should be sniffing the wind like some be-whiskered and apprehensive old shell-back commanding a becalmed wind-jammer when I was aboard an Ocean Weather Ship jam-packed with the most modern weather-divining instruments, but a visceral sensation was uncoiling in my belly.

Above me the navigational radar scanner rotated with its soft whirr and far above that, at the top of the ugly lattice mast, the huge apparatus of the Type 244 tracking array made a creaking noise as Cordwainer's people put it through its paces prior to the imminent balloon ascent.

Then I heard it, a low soughing through the criss-crossed girders of that steel monstrosity of a foremast. Quickly looking over the side I noticed the ship's deck lights caught the small but suddenly active little wavelets.

Some years before, when I had been on long leave after a ten-month voyage, I had been crewing in a friend's yacht. We had been lying at anchor in a Norwegian fjord at night. It had been calm and windless and I had gone on deck partly to check the anchor and also to have a pee over the side. Overhead the stars had burned bright, for although it was June it proved a chilly night. I went below and climbed back into my warm bunk. I had just been dropping off to sleep when there was a terrific bang, the yacht trembled from end-to-end and lay over on her beam ends.

We all scrambled out of our bunks, thinking we had been run down, but no water was coming in. Instead the wind was absolutely screaming through our rigging. We had been hit by a katabatic squall.

No such phenomenon could hit us out here in the ocean; katabatic squalls were a feature of mountainous coastlines, but something was out there cooking. I could see few birds about and by the time I turned to return to speak to Ted on the intercom, the wind was perceptible.

'Hello Ted…'

'Go ahead, Jamie.'

'We've got a rising wind up here alright…' I looked again at the anemometer. 'It's already up to…'

'Southerly, eight to ten knots.' Ted finished the observation for me.

'Looks like we're in for a blow, then,' chipped in Cordwainer from his radar control station on the deck below.

'Seems so.'

By the time Pennington relieved me the wind had risen to about fifteen knots. Not much yet, but hardening. That is to say there was no fluky uncertainly about it, it was increasing slowly but steadily as one watched and waited. By the time I had handed over to Charles and told him of the probability of a good blow, we had twenty-five knots.

He grinned at me over his mug of tea. 'Good-oh,' he said. I happened to know that unlike me and every other member of the ship's company, he had had no Christmas mail. I knew because there had been none for him in his pigeon-hole in the ward-room. The prospect of the sudden onset of a gale that might render Christmas pretty miserable was a blow, though he seemed cheered by the idea.

' "Long foretold, long last," ' I quoted, ' "Short notice, soon past." '

'Maybe not this time, Jamie, eh?' he said, still grinning and confirming my surmise.

'How d'you know?' I asked, slightly irritated, 'did you have a look at the sea-weed on the Met. Office door?'

He chuckled. 'Don't have to go that far. I can feel it in my water.'

'Chrissakes,' I said, then recollected something that I ought to tell him.

'We had a couple of alarms during the watch. A Panamanian tramp, at least I assume she was a tramp, they usually are, declared a Mayday then cancelled.'

'That's a bit odd.'

'That's what I thought, but...'

'Did you tell the Old Man?' Pennington interrupted.

'No, didn't bother since she cancelled almost as soon as she transmitted it.'

'Fair enough. Any idea how far away?'

'Not really, but got the idea it was not that far. She came through loud and clear.'

'And the second.' I told him about the Dutch air-liner. 'Okay…nothing else?'

'No, only the rising wind.'

He stood up, put his mug down on the tray and stretched. 'I have the ship, then. I suggest you get some beauty sleep. You'll be called before long…'

'Why,' I protested, not wishing my well-earned kip to be any more disturbed than it was likely to be with the onset of a gale. 'It's only a bit of wind…'

'I'm not talking about the wind,' Pennington said. 'These things usually come along in threes.'

'Is this more of your magnetic theory?' I asked jokingly.

'I'm talking about alarums and excursions,' he said coldly.

I was half-way down through the hatch when Pennington called me. 'Jamie..!'

'Yup?'

'Would you nip to my cabin and bring me my cigarette lighter. I've left it on my bunk-shelf?'

'Aye, aye.'

I had been in Pennington's cabin once or twice, but he did not 'entertain' in it as most of us did at one time or another. It was almost bare: no photographs, a few books on his bookshelf with another on his bunk-shelf beside the dull silver gleam of his cigarette lighter. Curious though I was about the man, I felt any lingering would be an intrusion and, in any case, he was waiting for me to take the lighter back up topside. As I picked it up (it was an expensive Dunhill), I glanced at the book lying beside it, noticing its title: *The Cruel Sea* by Nicholas Monsarrat.

It was not so much a mischievous curiosity that compelled me to pick the book up, it was more the fact that it had its original dust-wrapper and this under a plastic preserver. Once a red-hot best-seller that had made its author's fortune, it was a favourite book of mine, but I had not read it for years and my own copy (at home) was second-hand, lacking its original jacket. Solely out of a bibliophilic interest, and not a prurient intrusion of Pennington's personal effects, I flipped it open. The fly-leaf was bare, and I turned to see its publishing history, pretty certain that it was a first edition. I didn't get that far for under the author's name and above that of his publisher, Cassell, was a scrawled message: 'To Lt. Cdr C,P,R. Pennington DSC* RN, from his friend the author, Nicholas Monsarrat.

I almost felt that I had had my fingers burned. I replaced the book, picked up the lighter and clambered back up to the bridge. He thanked me for my 'kindness' and remarked that he would 'see me before cock-crow.'

I was not ready to process the information I had just then gleaned from my visit to his cabin, my mind rejecting it as though I had discovered some dirty secret about the man. Instead, as I cleaned my teeth and turned in I found my thoughts dominated by my return to the bridge and his facetious remark about seeing me before cock-crow. I assumed he was alluding to his assurance that his 'alarums and excursions' came in threes. Again I wondered if I ought not to have mentioned the Soviet spy-ship. Would that have constituted a first in the trio? I wished later that I had; combined with Pennington's magnetic theory it might have averted what happened that joyless Christmas.

4

Although neither of us had mentioned it during that midnight hand-over, it was now Christmas Eve. As I turned in I briefly recalled the inscription in Pennington's copy of Monsarrat's famous novel. At the very least it revealed that Pennington had served in the Royal Navy, either during the Second World War or the Korean War and that during that time he had done two things of note, for they didn't give a Distinguished Service Cross and Bar for sharpening the chart-room pencils. Anyway I filed the information away and tried to sleep.

And that miserable bloody night his prophecy proved accurate.

I must have been asleep for about an hour-and-a-half when I was woken up once again with water sluicing over me. The ship was heaving all over the place, rolling heavily but pitching and, worse still, pounding – smashing her bows down into water so solid that not only did it flood out much of the accommodation, but actually set-in the ship's forward shell-plating an inch, which caused a mirror in the ratings' wash-place under the flare of the bow, to be sprung out of its fastenings.

Outside, in the long fore-and-aft alleyway several inches of water sloshed up and down, cabin doors were open and their occupants peered out with expressions that varied from exasperation to terror, for it had been the crash and shudder of the impact that had woken some of them.

I dressed and went up to the bridge. Captain Gordon was

already up there and Mackenzie too. We had been caught in an enormous cross-sea, for the ship was under way, steering into the wind, but labouring over a swell some fifty degrees to the right of the wind-sea. I could hardly believe the deterioration in the conditions since I had left the bridge. In under two hours the wind had picked up to Storm Force 10 or 11 and it showed no sign of abating. The Old Man and Mackenzie were standing at the wheel-house windows, staring out into the darkness. They seemed idle observers at first; I was to learn differently a few minutes later.

Every few minutes, as the bow dug itself in and the ship shuddered with the effort of throwing off the green seas breaking over the rails, sheets of spray, driven down-wind at speed rattled on the armoured glass.

I made my way quietly into the chart-room. Pennington was at the chart-table putting down a LORAN fix. I looked at the barograph; the inky line of the stylus had fallen almost vertically since that initial movement just before midnight.

Pennington straightened up and looked round. 'Ah, it's you…'

'Yes. You were right.'

'Yes, I was, wasn't I? And there's more bad news,' he said, manipulating the parallel rules and dividers.

'Oh?'

'I'll tell you in a minute.' He went out into the wheel-house and I heard him say: 'One hundred and seven miles, two-three-eight true, sir. Well inside the grid.'

I also heard Duncan Gordon grunt acknowledgement, then Pennington was back behind the door curtain.

'Your Panamanian,' he said accusingly. 'She's on fire and has retransmitted her Mayday. No-one else is within miles…or if they are, they aren't saying. They,' meaning Captain Gordon and Mackenzie, 'are discussing what's to be done.'

And as though on cue, the curtain swept back a second time and Captain Gordon entered the chart-room. He sized both of us up. 'Weel gentlemen,' he said in his quiet voice, 'it looks as though our Christmas is goin' tae be post-poned. Perhaps nae a bad thing, given this weather.'

He picked up the intercom. 'Bridge to Comms. Captain speaking…'

'Comms. Bridge. All attention, sir.'

'FRAE MAISTER OCEAN WEATHER SHIP ON STATION INDIA,' Gordon dictated, 'TO MAISTER *SUNSHINE VICTORY*. YOOR MAYDAY ACKNOWLEDGED STOP AM COMING TO YOOR ASSISTANCE AT BEST SPEED STOP WILL SEND ECHO TANGO ALPHA IN ONE HOUR STOP ENDS… That'll do fur now, Comms.

'Very good, sir.'

'Did you copy Radar and Met.?'

Radar. Bridge. Copied, sir.'

'Met. Bridge. Copied, sir.'

'All other routines as usual.'

'All other routines as usual, sir.'

Gordon turned to us. 'The First Officer's bringing her roond to her new course now. It's dead to windward at the moment, though I suspect the wind'll veer and maybe give us a chance to get to her.' He paused and wiped his tired face with the palm of his right hand. I could hear the bristles of his chin rasp, a sort of accompaniment to the lonely anxiety of command. 'She sounds like an old Yankee Victory-ship,' he said.

'That's what I thought, sir,' said Pennington.

'Some more details would be helpful,' Gordon ruminated. 'Nae sign o' that bluidy glass rising yet, then?'

'No, sir. Not yet,' Pennington said before asking, 'Will you be flashing up another boiler, sir?'

'No, I dinna think we gain much advantage frae more steam in this sea, but you can put the engine-room in the picture jus' now.'

'Aye, aye, sir.' Pennington went out into the wheel-house, to the engine-room telephone.

Captain Gordon grunted and stared at me, as though weighing me up. 'Well, we will see wha' we shall see when we see it,' the Old Man said philosophically. 'You'd better get below and see if ye can grab some mair shut-eye.'

I had forgotten my wet-bunk and spent the remainder of that long and uncomfortable night on the long ward-room settee in company with Ted Wilkins, Jasper Cordwainer and the Chief Steward.

*

All I remember of the morning watch that followed was a dreary bash to windward. The wind was veering all the time, so from a violent pitching the overwhelming motion slowly metamorphosed into long and terrifying rolls, some of which laid us right over so that one's heart leapt into one's mouth for fear of a capsize. Sleet and snow-squalls blew through, raising the wind-speed from around Force 9 to 10, 11, even 12. One gust that I actually observed on the anemometer reached 97 knots and the surface of the Atlantic was white with spume.

As always with this wind speed the entire surface of the sea was, so-to-speak, sliced off, filling the air with atomised water-droplets thick with salt. Nevertheless, as the wind and sea crept slowly round towards the starboard beam, we were able to make more speed. Cautiously I rang on more revolutions, a few at a time, and only once had to take them off again for a while. The plot showed the general increase in our speed of advance: 6, 7 then 8 knots; we began to eat up those 107 miles.

We hunkered down in the wheel-house, McGrigor doing his long trick on the wheel with a stoicism I had to admire and poor little Hamish brazening it out miserably, only too happy for an excuse to go below for more tea, or milk, as we binged the hours away like tannin addicts. I recall he returned after one foray, triumphant with biscuits.

Captain Gordon came on the bridge at noon, partly, I think, to see that the balloon was launched successfully and no-one was lost off the after deck – for our routine duty went on as usual – and partly to see how we were getting on in our approach to the *Sunshine Victory*. We passed our Noon Position to the Comms. Office, along with an ETA of 17.30.

At this point there was not much more to be learned about the casualty beyond the occasional report from the Comms. Office that she was still afloat and still on fire. When I handed over at 12.30, Pennington advised me to try and get some sleep and: 'Get yourself back up here about 16.30. That's when I reckon the fun will start.'

I did as he advised. I hadn't thought I slept at all, except I do remember waking up a bit bemused. Slowly I caught hold of the reality again. I had jammed myself into my still damp bunk – we had a technique of shifting the inboard edge of the mattress up onto the lee-board so that we lay in a 'vee' caused by the mattress and the ship's side – and while a practical solution to sleeping, it made getting out of one's bunk difficult, a matter of timing with the ship's roll.

I don't think that I had thought of it before - or if I had, not with the intensity I had now to focus upon it - that a possibility existed that we might have to use one of the boats. And if we did, it was my job to take it away. To be candid, I was not sure that I wanted to do this, given the wind and sea-state. On the other hand I did not wish to be thought either inadequate to the task or a coward. Presciently I considered Pennington would not baulk at the assignment; indeed, I concluded he would relish it.

I had no idea what Captain Gordon had in his mind; perhaps,

like I was beginning to wish, he would be happy if the *Sunshine Victory* had burnt herself out and sunk by the time we reached her position. But why should she sink? She could burn and float. In this wind the fire might be confined to one end of the vessel; maybe that was what had happened earlier, that her cancelled Mayday meant her crew were tackling a fire that they had, as-it-were, corralled in the fore, or after part of their ship. Now, perhaps, matters had got further out of hand. Even so, waiting for fifteen or so hours for help to come was a tall order…

These were my thoughts as I clambered awkwardly out of my bunk, had a quick wash and cleaned my teeth. Although I dressed in uniform, I did so with care, exchanging black shoes for sea-boots and woollen stockings. Subconsciously or otherwise, I was dressing for duty beyond standing on the bridge. I checked my oil-skins, belt and Green River knife, leaving them handily available in my cabin.

By the time I got on the bridge things were a little clearer. Although howling about the bridge structure with a malicious note, the anemometers showed a drop in the average wind-speed. It was down to Force 9, and only gusting 10 at times. An improvement to be sure, and a welcome one, but my inward counsel wanted more.

In the wheel-house I joined Captain Gordon, First Officer Mackenzie and the Bosun. Patched-through to the Comms. Office as we were, we heard the radio traffic – now in plain speech over the radio-telephone – as we drew nearer.

'Come quick,' a voice kept repeating, at which the duty radio operator assured the *Sunrise Victory* that we were coming as fast as we could. After a while the terror and near hysteria of the wretched transmitter was such that Gordon turned the loud-speaker down. Meanwhile Pennington, was searching the sea-clutter dotting the screen of the navigational radar for the firm echo of the *Sunshine Victory*.

'Anything yet, Mr Pennington?' asked Gordon, betraying his anxiety.

'Not yet, sir,' came the cool response.

He turned to me. 'Go and ha'e a look at that barograph, Mr Childe.'

The Old Man's use of our surnames bespoke the seriousness of the situation. I did as I was bid. I knew what was going on in the Captain's mind, the constant slow veering in the wind suggested the approach of a cold front. Whether it would come sooner or later was now crucial and I stared at the thin inked line drawn by the instrument's stylus. It had certainly stopped falling, but the scale of the thing did not allow me to gauge whether its descent was flattening out.

I picked up the intercom. 'Met. Bridge calling.'

'Met. Bridge…'

'We're trying to see what the local barometric pressure is doing. Not much of a clue from our instruments up here. Can you give us any better info.'

'Stand-by…' I waited, then the voice came back, 'I'd put my money on it starting to level; it's certainly no longer falling.'

'Roger that. Many thanks.'

I returned to the wheel-house. 'I contacted Met., sir. They say it has definitely stopped falling and they'd put money on a levelling out being on its way.'

'Very good.'

For fifteen more minutes the *Weather Guardian* bashed her way to windward, then Pennington said, 'Jamie, get a fix, will you, we're about to move into a new grid-square. I again did as I was told and then transmitted the new grid-square letters to the Comms. Office. Five more minutes passed, then two more…'

'I've got something, sir!' Pennington's voice was triumphant. 'Two or three degrees on the port bow, eight miles away.'

'We're no goin' tae see her in this,' remarked Mackenzie, as a fresh squall bore down on us with a shrieking of the gale.

But the news had prompted Captain Gordon into action. 'Plot your tairget, Mr Pennington, just tae confirm she's stopped…'

'Already in hand, sir,' Pennington responded.

'Right, Iain, away wi' ye. Call out the hands and get the boats ready. But dinna lower them to the deck yet. Then get yersel' back up here.'

Captain Gordon went to the engine-room telephone and asked for the Chief Engineer to ring him back. Then he filled his pipe and lifted his binoculars to search the horizon ahead. I did not hear his conversation with the engine-room. Thinking to make myself useful, I grabbed my own and went out on the lee bridge-wing. The steel baffles that ran round the navigating bridge did a fair job of forcing the gale up and over our heads, sufficiently so to allow one to use a pair of glasses or take a sight. At first I could see nothing but the grey curtains of rain that hung from the sky and arrived as a million droplets on the wheel-house windows. Even through the revolving Kent clear-view screen the view was one of unrelieved monochrome. The ship was riding a little easier now, though her rolling had increased again and the thought of lowering boats, let alone recovering them, filled me with an uncomfortably visceral apprehension.

The minutes ticked by. I don't know how fast we were going, but we cannot have been making much more than 7 or 8 knots. Having estimated the visibility, I was mentally calculating the time before we might reasonably expect to sight the *Sunrise Victory* and concluded it would take at least another ten long minutes. My arms were beginning to ache, holding the heavy Barr & Strouds up to my eyes. They too were beginning to tire.

Then I saw the casualty: a small orange glow showing through the wet murk. 'I have her visual, sir!' I called in to the wheel-house, 'very fine on the port bow!'

I heard Gordon say, 'casualty in sight, Mr Pennington. I'll

take her from here…'

'Aye, aye, sir,' I heard Pennington reply, before giving his concluding report. 'Distant three point two miles, sir.'

From that moment things began to happen very quickly.

*

As I turned back into the wheel-house, Iain Mackenzie came up from the boat-deck and Pennington emerged from behind the curtain screening the navigational radar. Captain Gordon turned to the three of us and looked from one to the other, as though appraising us for the first time. I had never previously realised how a crisis such as the one we were now involved in affected men so differently. All my training suggested, by its bland presumptions, that all would go as planned; that, armed with one's own doughty courage, one followed a sort of drill ensuring all would be well. Like most young officers I had run through emergencies in my head, if only for the oral examinations at which we were supposed to convince the examiner – who held our entire future in the palms of his hands – that we were all heroic members of the Bulldog breed. Few of us thought of the possibility of panicking and even if we did, the examination room was not the place to lose one's nerve.

Now I stood there, undergoing Captain Gordon's scrutiny. I was the ship's boat officer. Whether I liked it or not, it was my duty to take the boat away if he ordered it. Having stared round at us he said, 'I'm goin' tae call the casualty, gentlemen…' and turned away to pick up the VHF Radio handset.

'*Sunrise Victory*, *Sunrise Victory*, *Sunrise Victory*, this is the British Ocean Weather Ship *Weather Guardian* calling on Channel Sixteen. Come in *Sunrise Victory…*'

There was no response, then Pennington took a call from the Comms. Office. Turning to the Old Man he said, 'there's been no sound from the casualty on R/T for the last seven minutes, sir. Comms. thinks they've been driven off the bridge…'

There was a strange crackle on the VHF and although it was on loud-speaker, Gordon pressed the hand-set to his ear. We all heard the words, broken-up by interference: 'Come quick, come quick… Fire bad…very bad…boats lost…Captain dead…'

Gordon hung up. 'Right,' he said, 'if we're going tae rescue any of these poor bastards we're going tae need twa boats; that's you Mr Pennington and you Mr Childe. Ah'm lookin' tae ye not to tak' any stupid risks and nae bluidy heroics. Act like good and prudent seamen…' he was not looking at me at this point, but fixing Pennington with a meaningful, even a baleful glare. 'Ah want both boats back in one piece…'

I could understand Captain Gordon's concern; the two motor-boats were not just the ship's life-boats, they were working boats, required for rescue work such as we were about to undertake, but not to be thrown away on a single operation. Theoretically there might be another tomorrow.

'Iain,' Gordon went on, 'get one of the boys tae drop a small amount of colza oil in the seamen's heads ready to flush intae the watter, then stand-by the boats with all available hands.' He turned to Pennington and myself. 'Away doon and get yersel's suitably dressed and then get back up here and I'll tell ye what Ah intend doin'…'

'Aye, aye, sir,' we all responded as Mackenzie disappeared out through the lee door and Pennington and I scrambled down the vertical ladder to our respective cabins.

As I had furthest to go, I was last back on the bridge and I was conscious I had kept the others waiting, for which I apologised.

'Reet,' said the Old Man, 'now this is what Ah intend doin'…' Captain Gordon's instructions were explicit and in some odd way I felt safe in his hands, even though I was about to leave the safety of the ship and a great deal depended on my own actions.

I shot a glance at Mackenzie; his face was a mask. Then I

glanced at Pennington. What there was of his face visible above his great grey beard was ashen. This astonished me; here was a man decorated for conspicuous action in war, not once but twice; moreover, I knew him as an irrepressible character, one who literally laughed – and indeed sang – in the face of a hurricane-force wind! Surely it was not fear I read in his eyes? I found the very thought disquieting. This sort of thing was new to me; it did me no good at all to see an experienced man like Pennington quail.

I set the thought aside; I had my duty to do; I needed to focus…

'So,' Captain Gordon was saying, 'No. 2 Boat first, that'll be you Mr Childe… That's all, gentlemen,' Captain Gordon concluded. 'And guid luck to ye.'

As Gordon turned away to pick-up his binoculars and study the casualty, we three moved off the bridge and down the after ladders to the boat-deck. Once there Mackenzie drew us into a huddle. 'Ah'm nae lowerin' the boats to the rail fust. We're likely tae roll heavily. You'll go straight fra' the stowed position intae the watter. Understood?'

'Aye.'

'Aye.'

'Let's awa' then.'

I pulled my life-jacket on and did it up securely, hefted my portable VHF radio-telephone onto one shoulder then clambered up into the port boat. Colin Buchanan was already there, along with several seamen and the boy Hamish.

'Who told you to get in the boat, Hamish?'

'Nae-one…sir.'

I leaned over the gunwhale and hailed Mackenzie. 'I've a Deck-boy in my boat, sir. D'you want me to send him back on deck?'

'Dinna dae that, sir!' Hamish squealed, adding, as if it would make a difference, 'Ah brought the blankets.'

'If he wants tae go, keep him,' Mackenzie called up to me.

'D'you want to go, Hamish?'

He looked at me and then at McGrigor up in the boat's bow. 'Ay, Ah dae, sir.'

'Very well. Get forrard and assist McGrigor.'

Mackenzie called up to ask if we were ready. I took a quick look round the boat. Everyone's life-jacket seemed well secured. 'Is the plug in?' I asked.

'Aye, Jamie,' said Buchanan.

'Okay. Are you ready to swing that handle?'

'Aye.' A non-starting engine would be a bloody disaster.

'All ready, sir!' I sang out.

From the engine-room skylight I heard the telegraph jangle and felt the *Weather Guardian* increase speed. The second boiler had been flashed-up, I realised, and was now being called upon in earnest. Standing at the stern of No. 2 Boat I was almost as high as the bridge and for the first time I looked around me. I could not see the casualty, which was obscured by the bridge super-structure but a pall of black smoke lay on the water, being torn to leeward by the gale. Although we were the lee boat, the sea all around us remained streaked with white spume as the gale howled in the masts, the aerials, the stays, funnel guys and halliards. I could see the top of Captain Gordon's head as he stood on the port bridge wing, giving orders to the helmsman, watching his approach to the *Sunrise Victory* and keeping an eye on our preparations.

From the engine-room skylight I heard the telegraph jangle and felt the *Weather Guardian* increase speed. She vibrated with the power as Gordon turned her first a little to starboard, exposing the casualty to my line of sight. The *Sunrise Victory* was suddenly quite close, a black and white shape rolling violently in the trough of the sea, more than half her length ablaze. She seemed set against a cloud of black smoke and I could see the whole of her port and windward side. The two lifeboats were on fire in their davits. I could also see a black huddle of men on her poop.

We were now surging past her at a rate of knots. Surely the Old Man wasn't about to launch my boat at such a speed? Then, as we drew past the sharp bow of the Victory-ship with her high fo'c's'le, the telegraphs rang again and the *Guardian*'s motion changed as the helm was put hard over to port. Gordon swung her to pass the bow of the *Sunrise Victory*, yelling to Mackenzie: 'No. 2 Boat away!'

'Gripes away!' Mackenzie bellowed and I felt the boat move, then its keel swung out of the chocks as the ship rolled.

'Start her up!' I told Colin Buchanan.

'Lower away!' Mackenzie commanded.

The davits, hinged at the ship's rail, began to swing outwards; as soon as they hit the stops the wire falls – which controlled this outboard traverse – continued to run out and we descended from the davit head. The engine coughed into life as we passed deck level and jerked down the ship's side, banging the skids on the inward roll.

But by turning hard and fast, Captain Gordon had thrown the ship's stern up, into the wind-sea, creating a 'smooth' alongside. This was enhanced by the dribble of colza oil from forward. And by not lying directly across the path of the oncoming seas, Gordon had minimised the ship's roll.

We hit the water with a crash that jerked the teeth in our skulls, the falls fell slack, then jerked tight again, before the boat was properly afloat. 'Leggo blocks!' I shouted. Up in the bow McGrigor dealt with the forward block while I struggled for a few seconds before getting the after one clear. Above me Mackenzie ordered the falls drawn into the ship's side to prevent the heavy blocks stunning and concussing anyone of the boat's crew.

'Leggo forrard!' I bellowed and McGrigor cast off the toggle painter. We were on our own.

'Full ahead!' I said to Colin as I grabbed the tiller. We had to get away from the ship's side before her leeway pressed down on us, or any increase in speed drew us in, under the rise and fall of her stern to have us chopped to match-wood by the screw. But Gordon was at the top of his game; increasing speed with a double ring on the telegraph, he continued his port turn, the *Guardian*'s stern swung away from us, struck a breaking sea and sent a sheet of water high into the air on the far quarter as I turned No. 2 Boat inside the ship's turning-circle and headed for the *Sunrise Victory*.

I took no notice of further movements of the *Guardian*, knew nothing of the launch of No. 1 Boat; it was on the far side of the ship anyway and the Old Man was swinging her round to lay another 'smooth'. As the first away, the honours lay with us as we ran down towards the *Sunrise Victory* perhaps half a mile from us. That may sound a good distance, but as sea five cables – half a nautical mile – is close, especially in such conditions as we now found ourselves. On the other hand, although in a tiny boat surrounded by a howling wilderness of wild water, our cockle-shell 'swam' well. She shipped no solid water, only a little spray, despite her freeboard being less than two feet and I found that I could steer her with little trouble.

It was now time to turn my attention to what lay ahead.

So skilfully had Captain Gordon position the *Weather Guardian* for our launch, and so smoothly had that process gone, that we were soon almost directly in the lee of the wallowing hull. Our first problem was the pall of smoke which was dense, black, foul and hot, and lay on the surface of the sea. To get to the men on the poop of the *Sunrise Victory* we had to pass through this and I called out to the boat's crew to keep their heads down. They obeyed to a man, which left only me exposed to the noxious bloody stuff as I steered No. 2 Boat through the filthy cloud as quickly as possible, gasping for breath.

Fortunately we emerged unscathed quite quickly, but found ourselves much closer to the side of the burning ship and wrapped in an intense heat. I had a fleeting impression of missing lifeboats on the starboard side, and paint blistering everywhere even as I put the tiller over and we swung up towards the stern of the casualty.

Only the poop was as yet unaffected and seemed crowded with men, men who were terrified, and with good reason, for the fire was vicious in its intensity and we could feel its scorching heat one hundred yards away. I had no idea how we were going to help those men, but they solved that problem for me, clambering over the rails to drop into the sea. Some had lifejackets, others didn't. Some had warm clothing, some didn't. Some could swim, others couldn't. What they had in common was fear. What we learned a few minutes later was their fear was a mortal dread and it soon affected us.

I took No. 2 Boat close up, under the stern where the ship's name and her port of registry were painted in white on her dark grey hull.

'Stop her, Colin,' I said. We began pulling the poor devils inboard as quickly as we could. It is far from easy to pull a man aboard a boat over a gunwhale, no matter how low in the water the boat is, or how keen is the individual to co-operate. It was, in short, back-breaking labour. All I can really say is that that handful of Scots seamen were incredible in their endeavours. But even this was not enough for everyone. One survivor tried to jump directly into the boat. He just missed little Hamish and landed across the gunwhale. He must have broken his back in an instant, although Hamish grabbed him and, with an access of strength only the moment could have lent him, pulled him into the boat's bilge where he lay utterly senseless. The others, some burned, some wide-eyed with absolute terror, either fell supine into the bottom of the boat, or clawed their way aft towards me – a sight I shall never forget.

'Give out those blankets, Hamish,' I remember yelling.

'Ah'm doin' that noo,' the boy shouted back, in high indignation, but it was what was being shouted at me by the survivors that had the greater impact.

The message was conveyed to me in several modes, the clearest of which was: 'Ship explode! Ship explode!'

'You have explosives on board?' I asked, my heart travelling remorselessly up my gullet.

'Ja! Ja!' said one. 'Si! Si!' said another. 'We've eighty tons of the stuff…' the Yankee accent came through.

'Jesus Christ!'

The boat was already dangerously full, yet there were still men coming over the rail, along with those too terrified to do anything, who remained rooted to the spot.

I bent over and said to Colin Buchanan. 'Go astern, we're too close.' Straightening up I looked round for the other boat. At first I could see nothing of her. It flashed across my mind that Pennington had been genuinely scared, that he was hanging back deliberately, letting me and my boat's crew run all the risks.

Then I was aware of No. 1 Boat roaring towards us. Pennington stood bolt upright in the stern, his big fist on its tiller, his beret at its jaunty angle, his head poised so that his beard seemed to point in the direction he wished his boat to proceed. He closed us rapidly, ranging up alongside us to port and giving me a salute.

'How many have you picked up?' he called out.

'No idea, about twenty or so…'

'Can't be above another twenty at most,' he said, looking up at the stern of the *Sunrise Victory* as it rose and fell, threatening to bear down upon us as we too felt the motion of the sea. 'Get your lot back to the ship. I'll bring the rest.'

No. 1 Boat was passing us now as she moved in under the stern of the casualty, just as we were backing off and gathering stern-way. In other circumstances it would have been the seamanlike thing to do. But unlike No. 1 Boat we were pulling out from the ship's lee and already the seas were breaking dangerously close to us. One threw us almost on our beam ends before I got her head round, all the while trying to tell Pennington that the *Sunrise Victory* had explosives on board.

I tried shouting at him, but he was concentrating on his own work, In the end all I could do was to take a full turn to starboard, before again coming up on *his* port-quarter. This threatened to destroy all semblance of order aboard my boat, for the more active of the survivors were horrified to find us turning back towards the *Sunrise Victory*. One tried to shove me away from the tiller, another to dislodge Colin from his post crouching over the diesel engine.

As I came up alongside Pennington he became aware of me and turned on me angrily. 'Fuck off back to the ship, for Christ's sake!'

'Not before I tell you…' at this point I was obliged to ward-off another assault by a frightened seaman, '…that I'm told she has explosives on board!'

Pennington stared at me for a split-second before shouting, 'I fucking knew it!' Turning away from me he roared: 'Come on you bastards, jump! Jump! Jump for Chrissakes!'

Then without looking at me he called out, 'Away you go Jamie! Away you go! And tell the ship!'

Colin Buchanan did not wait for my order; he had already jerked the gear lever astern willy-nilly. It was nearly the end of us, for the boat was over-loaded with nearly thirty survivors on board when we actually counted them, and we gained rather too much stern-way. I was in the act of fiddling with my portable radio-telephone and had to relinquish the tiller momentarily. With the stern-way, the rudder slammed over and the tiller swung across the boat, striking me sharply on the arm.

The pain made me feel sick but somehow I got a message away to the *Weather Guardian*, advising Captain Gordon to stand off, for fear of an explosion. When my head had cleared and I had mastered myself again I found we were half-way back to the ship towards which I had been steering all the time.

While most in the boat stared astern, at the blazing hulk of the *Sunrise Victory*, I must needs concentrate on the business of recovery. I knew that lowering a boat in heavy seas is difficult, but conventional lifeboats are crudely designed for just that, a one-way trip off their parent vessel. Being picked-up is entirely another matter, from the manoeuvring of the mother-ship, by way of the extremely dangerous (for those who have to do it) hooking on of the blocks, through to the lifting out of the water. If one block became disengaged during a few crucial seconds – quite possible if and when a sea lifted the entire boat so that the wire falls went slack – one end of the boat could drop and throw people into the sea. Even when both blocks are secured, a sudden lift of the boat by a sea beneath it which then falls away, can threaten the actual structure of the boat. And although certified for a large number of persons, once again, the design of the boat was for a one-way trip; the falls could be let go and the boat was free of them, free to escape as a *life*-boat. What we were about to attempt was the reverse. The lifting and sudden drop was not merely a matter of chance, as of a sea rising up under the boat, but was a compound of this and the rolling of the recovering ship.

Again, the problem of the mother-ship's attitude *vis-à-vis* the wind and sea would be crucial. At my oral examinations for competence as a deck officer, I would have uttered, with an air of confident bravado, the simple maritime cliché: 'make a lee.' But a lee in the open ocean is not such an easy thing to do, for even with a little ship with as low a profile as the *Weather Guardian*, a Force 8 or 9 drove her to leeward at anything up to 4 knots – faster than a fit man can walk normally. This could press down upon the lifeboat alongside, sometimes making extreme difficulties for the boat's crew when compounded by the ship's roll.

All these things flashed through my mind as we closed with the *Guardian* and I tried to recall Captain Gordon's instructions. I had no idea then how long ago he had given them, but it seemed an age, for Einstein is right, time is *not* a constant, especially when the human body and mind are under an excess of unnatural strain.

The ship was turning towards us as we bucked and rolled and the VHF Radio-telephone crackled into life. I recognised Iain Mackenzie's voice with a huge sense of relief, as though he had physically thrown me a lifeline.

'*Weather Guardian* to Number Two Boat, stop and maintain your position. I repeat, stop and maintain your position. Acknowledge.'

'Stop and maintain my position. Roger.' I responded.

I nodded at Buchanan. 'Just give me steerage, Colin,' I said as I began a feverish few minutes meeting the breaking seas. The wind noise remained tremendous and up on the crests as they burst and seethed around us it was a mixture of the sublime and the hellish. Then we would dip into the long troughs, broken it is true by lesser waves, but divided from the horror of those tumbling wave-crests by the huge intervals of the oceanic swells.

It was another curiosity of our situation that the higher wind speeds that we had experienced during the earlier part of that

Christmas Eve had cut off these crests, turning them into a fine spume as I have already mentioned. Although this produced a mass of air moving with a terrific force against which we had had to motor, it flattened the actual sea. Now, as the wind dropped a tad, the sea was building up again – hence the breaking crests through which I was now constrained to navigate my frail little command with its lading of human souls.

And I gave them a brief look. My own seamen, bless them, bore expressions of rugged concentration. From McGrigor up forrard, whose sole job it would be to secure that forward davit fall to the hook in the boat's bow, to Colin Buchanan hunched over the thumping Thorneycroft diesel upon which all depended, seemed imbued with some extraordinary spirit, some co-operative endeavour that, we all hoped, would very shortly yield its own reward. That is, I think the only way that I can put it, for I was not idly regarding these men, including little Hamish, I was assessing them for the parts they must play in the following decisive minutes, seeking in them the vitality I must myself exert to accomplish our task.

And that lay in the others squatting nervously on the boat's thwarts or huddled in its bottom, the lucky ones wrapped in the blankets Hamish had handed out to them. They were a polyglot lot, the crew of that Panamanian tramp. Later I would find out their nationalities, from Americans – black and white - to Mexican *mestizos*, a Cuban, Five Sicilian Italians and several Chinese. They wore a variety of clothing; two of the white Americans obviously officers in a sort of uniform, two of the Chinese in the blue-and-white checked trews of cooks, three in the black trousers and white jackets of stewards, the remainder mostly the black men and the Hispanics in the non-descript dark dungarees and tee-shirts of engine-room greasers and firemen, or the heavier apparel of seamen.

What they had in common was faces that bore expressions of

extreme trauma. Only later did I discover that this motley-looking band had fought the fire heroically for hours; that they had thought to have overcome it – hence the cancellation of their May Day – before it broke out again with a raging ferocity they could not counter, exhausted as they were. Nevertheless, they had tried, and in trying several of their number had been killed, most horribly burned by all accounts. But all that came out later; in those few moments as I took stock all I was aware of was that somewhere behind me, where all *their* eyes seemed trans-fixed, was a floating bomb on the cusp of explosion.

But I had no time to worry about such things, for the *Weather Guardian* was coming down towards me at all of fifteen knots, just as she would have done as the *Weobley Castle* hunting a U-boat twenty years earlier. She was set to pass down the boat's port side, less than a cable away.

'Here she comes, boys,' I called out reassuringly. Some looked round; others ignored me. The experiences many of those survivors had endured in the last hours can only have aged them mentally and I must have appeared like some gauche youth, standing in the stern. I had lost my beret and my unruly hair snapped around my head. In one of those inconsequential moments that occur at such times of idle stress, as I waited for Captain Gordon to position the ship for our recovery, I was reminded of Pennington's possible characterisation of me as being *a deck ornament full of piss, epaulettes and no bottom*. It reminded me that we had yet to accomplish our mission.

The *Weather Guardian* seemed damned close as she came past us. I looked up at her bridge. There stood the Old Man, God bless him, his gaunt face regarding us; then his head turned. I saw his mouth open as he gave the order, though I could hear nothing above the scream of the wind, of course, and the strange swishing noise that was a combination of steam-power and a closely passing ship's wash.

Even as we watched the *Guardian* began her tight, U-boat killing turn, as her big spade rudder drove her stern away from us. I suddenly heard the homely jangle of the telegraph and was aware of Iain Mackenzie, the Bosun and the davit party at their posts, ready to pick us up.

Captain Gordon took her right round us, cutting that essential smooth in the water as one of Hamish's fellows continued to dribble colza oil out of the crew's heads forward. It was like a mother's encircling arm embracing her off-spring and it ended with a furious ringing of the telegraph as, down in the bowels of the ship the reversing gear was put-in.

'Now, Jamie!' Mackenzie bawled, but we were already in motion. Buchanan had increased the engine-revs as soon as I gave the word and I now ordered everyone except the boat's crew to hunker down.

During our absence from the ship, the Bosun and his handful of remaining seamen had been busy rigging boat-ropes for our recovery. These were stretched from forward to aft, looped up to the ship's rail by short rope called 'lizards,' at each of which a seaman stood.

As I brought No. 2 Boat in alongside, the davit blocks, although restrained at deck level, nevertheless swung out from the ship's side and then fell back against the shell-plating with a metallic bang as the *Guardian* rolled.

'Watch the stern-wash, Jamie!' Mackenzie called as I relinquished the tiller and made a grab for the boat-rope being offered me by the Able-seaman holding the after lizard and hanging over the ship's side as far as he dared. All around us the sea seethed a white and green marble, the result of Captain Gordon's crash-stop, pushing the stern of the boat away from the ship's side. This at least saved my head from the heavy swinging davit block as I grabbed the proffered boat-rope and caught a turn and then swiftly belayed it.

'All fast forrard!' sang out the indomitable McGrigor as he secured the other extreme of the boat.

'Forrard block!' said Mackenzie above us, as the Able-seaman who'd handled the forward lizard, moved aft and slackened off the loop retaining the wire fall and its lethal pulley-block.

I watched anxiously. It was imperative to get the forward bock secured first, but the whole operation must be accomplished as fast as possible. I was pleased to see that McGrigor had told Hamish to hold onto the waistband of his life-jacket with one hand, allowing him two hands to engage the hook.

'Hooked-in forrard!' from McGrigor.

'After block!' from Mackenzie above me and it was my turn to tussle with the heavy steel pulley. I felt a hand at my own waist and knew Buchanan was doing his duty. Sadly, in those days we had no patent releasing and connecting gear. Even so, it seems such a simple thing to hook in a block, but it took all my strength, twisting the thing and aligning it at the precise moment the boat rose sufficiently for me to get the connecting link over the pea of the hook. And even when I had it there and had holloaed my success to Mackenzie on the boat deck, I had to hold the damned thing in place as the boat rose and fell, the ship rolled and my fingers were at risk of annihilation. Moreover my bruised arm hurt and I could sense a sudden approaching weakness. The one thing I knew in those long seconds of struggle was: that I couldn't, *absolutely mustn't*, let that bloody link drop off the block!

When I had got the bastard thing located, and without looking up I bellowed for all I was worth: 'Hooked in!!'

'Hoist away!' from Mackenzie. The winch ground into life, the falls snapped taught, slackened again as the ship leaned over us and the blocks threatened to drop off, and then we were drawn upwards, out of the water. As we were bowsed into the ship's side I saw the Chief Steward and his motley lot armed with more blankets. We passed the survivors, some now trembling uncontrollably with cold, or fear, or released tension, onto the boat deck. I heard Iain Mackenzie asking who was the senior officer and as Colin Buchanan straightened up from his shut-down Thorneycroft I impulsively shook his hand.

'Well done, Colin,' I remember saying, grinning at him.

'Well done yersel' yer Sassenach bastard!' he replied cheerfully. We were elated and I thought it the finest compliment anyone had ever paid me.

Then Hamish called out, 'what dae we dae wi' this fella, sir?'

I turned. In my euphoria I had forgotten all about the poor bastad who had broken his back. McGrigor was bending over him. He looked up, shaking his head. 'He's dead, sir.'

Crestfallen, we got his broken body on deck and once the corpse was clear, I left McGrigor and another Able-seaman in the boat to see it hoisted right up and followed Hamish onto the deck.

'Well, did ye enjoy tha' wee Hamish?' Mackenzie, his eyes gleaming, asked the Deck-boy.

Hamish took his eyes off the dead man who was being carried aft. 'Aye, sir, Ah did, tho' Ah was a bit a-feared tae begin with.'

'We were all that, Laddie, an' we're nae all oot o' the woods yet…' He turned to me. 'Get yersel' up on the bridge, Jamie, there's hot tea up there. Gilshaw'll see tae this lot o' puir divils. You did well.'

I was divesting myself of my cumbersome life-jacket when Hamish caught my eye. He seemed to have grown three or four inches since he stepped aboard the boat, what? – I looked at my watch – nearly *three* hours ago!

I beckoned to him to follow me, over to the funnel and saw his face fall. Was the poor lad expecting a bollocking? It seemed so, for the truculent frown fell like a visor across his mush.

'You did very well, Hamish,' I said. 'I was very proud of the entire boat's crew, but you above all, for it was all very new to you.' I held out my hand and watched him change colour and expression like a red-haired chameleon.

'Thank'ee, sir,' he said without a trace of hesitation.

'In fact,' I added, 'on this afternoon's showing, you'd make a damned fine officer.'

*

Although my most immediate part of the rescue was over, as soon as I reached the bridge I realised that the whole enterprise was very far from over. The atmosphere remained tense, for Captain Gordon had rung on full speed and was giving orders to the helmsman from the port bridge-wing. Seeing me he said: 'Very well done, Mr Childe. Get yersel' a cuppa, then man the VHF… Ah've lost that bugger Pennington…'

In my own preoccupations I had not given Pennington another thought. Apart from the chief concern of getting No. 2 Boat safely back to the ship, was the extreme worry about the *Sunrise Victory* exploding, but even that horrendous possibility had shrunk, such is the ability of the human brain to compartmentalise under extreme conditions.

'Did you receive my message about the explosives, sir?'

'Aye.' The Old Man was curt; while I – in my junior capacity - had been dickering about with tactical decisions, he had had to hold in mind the bigger picture and he moved restlessly about the bridge like a big cat on the prowl: watching the ship and the sea, picking his moment before giving his helm orders and increasing or decreasing the ship's speed, and all the while scanning the sea for a sign of No. 1 Boat.

Just before I dived into the wheel-house for a cup of hot sweet tea I looked over at the *Sunrise Victory*. We were still to windward of her, but nonetheless she seemed enveloped in smoke. Judging by the angle of her masts and the top of her tall funnel, she now had quite a list but at the heart of what was left of her was that deep red glow which caught my eye earlier, oh, so much earlier, that long afternoon.

In the chart-room I found a large aluminium pot of tea and a clean mug. I was just pouring out my tea when the mug shook as a hot shock-wave passed right through the wheel-house and there occurred the most tremendous explosion.

'Jesus!' from me.

'Holy fuck!' from the helmsman.

I did not have time to be frightened; I was back in the wheel-house in an instant. The helmsman, Able-seaman Corrigan, was steadying himself and back on the wheel from which he had been thrown and slammed against the after bulkhead with the physical impact of the shock-wave.

'You okay?' I asked.

'Aye, sir.'

I don't know whether it was the shock-wave or the sea but the *Guardian* seemed to have taken a long roll to starboard (away from the casualty) and I seemed to struggle uphill to get the port wheel-house door open. I emerged onto the bridge-wing, into air which seemed to be thick with dust, or smoke, or something. There was no sign of Captain Gordon.

'The hellum is hard a-port, sir,' shouted Corrigan.

Christ! The ship! A single glance over my shoulder told me she was running at full speed, full speed on two boilers, and turning inwards towards the *Sunrise Victory*.

'Fuck! Fuck! Fuck! Fuck!' I stared through the murk which the gale was now clearing rapidly. 'Fuck Pennington too,' I thought as I screamed: ''Midships and steady her as she goes!'

Corrigan repeated the order as I closed the distance to the telegraph with the longest strides of my life and swung the handle to 'Slow'.

'Steady as she goes, sir,' Corrigan said, as though we were

coming up the Clyde with a westering sun over the Isle of Arran and Cloch Point lighthouse flashing on the starboard bow.

And that is when the sky began to rain debris on us.

*

What seemed like a thousand thoughts rushed through my dazed head even as we suffered under this cascade of wood and steel fragments. The clatter and crash of all this, and then the sudden *BANG!* as something serious carried away, broke through the ringing of my ears occasioned by the explosion. But I was far from steady on my feet and I was staggering about trying to clear my head. The first cogent thing that came to me was to focus on the safety of the ship. I was the only officer on the bridge; I had no idea what had happened to Captain Gordon, nor whether Iain Mackenzie and his deck-party had been swept overboard by the blast. No. 1 Boat was still out there somewhere, or – as seemed more likely – blown to smithereens; but I could not assume this, we must search for her. And if we – or I – found her, what then? How many men did I have to recover her; we might have to use scrambling nets instead of hoisting her, but how would we rig them without men to do it…?

I felt the tide of panic rising inexorably up my oesophagus and then the engine-room phone rang. I think it saved both me and the ship, for I grabbed it and answered.

'Wha' the fuck's going on?' It was the Chief Engineer on the control platform in the engine-room.

'The casualty has just exploded…'

'You're telling me? Christ! I thought we'd hit somethin' the concussion down here nearly knocked us all o'er, now we've got steel shite coming doon frae the skylight…'

'Sorry, Chief,' I said, as if I was personally responsible.

'Is that you Jamie?'

'Yes, Chief.'

'Can Ah speak wi' the Old Man?'

'I don't know where he is, Chief…'

'Well who the fuck's in charge up there?'

The question pulled me together. 'We're just assessing things,' I said, 'I'll give you a ring back in a moment or two.' And without waiting for an answer I hung up. I then rang the engine-room telegraph to 'Stop!' At least it looked as though someone was in charge.

In the next few minutes we somehow got a grip on the situation.

I stumbled out onto the starboard bridge-wing intending to walk the few steps aft and see if there was anyone left alive on the starboard boat-deck. In doing so I nearly tripped over Captain Gordon. It turned out that he had himself crossed through the wheel-house intending to see if Mackenzie was getting ready to recover No. 1 boat on the starboard side. In doing so he had left the sliding door open and it was this – along with the fact that the port door was already drawn-back – that allowed the blast and shock-waves to pass through the wheel-house, causing the minimum of damage and leaving the armoured glass windows intact.

I helped him drag himself into the wheel-house. He was badly cut about the head and I called Corrigan to leave the wheel and help me. Between us we got him propped up against the engine-room telegraph and the forward bulkhead.

'See if they're okay on the boat-deck…' he murmured.

'Just doing that, sir,' I said, standing up and telling Corrigan to put an intercom call for a first-aider to come to the bridge immediately. Then I ran to the after starboard bridge wing. Most of the heavy stuff seemed to have finished falling on us and it was light-weight crap that descended on us now. Even so I covered my head with my hands. It was only a matter of a few feet to my vantage point and when I got there I scanned the deck. Apart from a shower of wreckage it was empty!

I doubled back into the wheel-house as something struck my right shoulder. Corrigan was just replacing the intercom mike in its holder and I snatched it from his hand.

'Attention all hands! Bridge to ship's company. First Officer, Bosun or anyone from the boat-deck party report to the bridge NOW!'

I turned my attention back to Captain Gordon. He was hauling himself onto his feet.

'You'd better get into the chart-room, sir and sit on the settee. There's help coming.'

'The ship… The ship…' he mumbled.

'I've got the con, sir,' I replied with a great deal more confidence than I felt.

'She's rolling…'

'It's okay, sir…'

'We've two boilers…'

'I know,' I soothed him. I had forgotten and it didn't help that we were stopped. Any moment now the safety valve would lift, we'd vent steam with a blood-curdling shriek and the Chief would be ringing up to ask what the fucking hell we were doing now?

Once we had got the Captain onto the chart-room I jerked my head at Corrigan to get back on the wheel, then I rang on Slow-Ahead and steadied the ship. The Second Steward appeared uncertainly clambering up through the wheel-house hatch throwing his first-aid bag ahead of him.

'The Old Man's in the chart-room,' I said, picking up the Barr & Stroud binoculars. 'D'you know if the First Officer's okay?'

'Aye, they're all doon below, sorting the survivors oot.'

Survivors? Christ! I had forgotten all about them. No. 1 Boat was *my* next priority.

I went to the port-wheel house door. To this day I have no idea whatsoever how much time had passed since the *Sunrise Victory* blew herself into Kingdom Come, but she had gone, leaving, like Melville's *Pequod*, the sea to rolled on as it had done for countless thousands of years. All that remained of the ship was some wreckage, but I was anxious to see if any of this was the remains of No. 1 Boat or her poor bloody crew..

I reduced to Dead Slow and turned the *Guardian* in towards where I thought the *Sunrise Victory* had disappeared and – as the stock phrase had it – 'proceeded with caution'.

There was a great deal of debris but the swirl caused by the sinking ship was over-washed by the wind-sea, which tumbled the remains of her slowly downwind, for the gale had not one whit abated during all this horrible time. I could see nothing of any boat – a vain hope anyway in that roil of white water, my heart sinking. Perhaps, I thought in a moment of tardy inspiration, I should try the silent VHF.

Turning back into the wheel-house I picked-up the handset. I didn't bother with formalities, I simply called for No. 1 Boat to respond, but there was no reply.

It was at this point that Iain Mackenzie appeared on the bridge. He looked shattered, his face pallid, his hands shaking.

'Sorry it took me sae long, Jamie,' he said apologetically.

I learned later that he had managed to get all the survivors and my boat's crew on their way down below just as the *Sunrise Victory* went up. He had himself been steeping over the sea-step when the blast caught him, swung him round, striking him against the steel frame of the water-tight door.

I gave him a quick briefing, told him the Old Man was in the chart-room with a badly gashed head but that Bill, the Second Steward was attending to him. I then told him that I was taking the ship slowly down towards the position of the wreckage, trying to see what I could of the remains of No. 1 Boat. Mackenzie frowned, as if finding it difficult to hoist all this in.

'Oh, Christ! Pennington! Is he gone?'

'I don't know, sir.' I said.

'We must look fur him, Jamie, we must!' This with great emphasis, but I could see he was in terrible pain.

'Are you alright?' I asked.

'I'll dae…' he hesitated, unwilling to admit a weakness. 'It's ma fucking ribs, Ah think…'

'We'd better get you below…'

'Dinna fesh yersel' just yet. Later'll dae for that.' He drew some deep breaths. 'I'll take the con but ye'll hae to dae all the grunt work. Hae ye called Pennington of VHF?'

'Aye. No reply.'

'Ah think he took the duff set,' Mackenzie said, between his teeth. 'It's got an intermittent fault…'

'Shit…'

'Try him again, and keep trying every few minutes. Between that get oot there an' keep a guid lookout.'

'Aye, aye, sir.'

'Ah'll hae a wee peek at the radar…'

I did as I was bid as Mackenzie stopped the ship. She began to broach then roll and roll. I tried very trick I knew to quarter the sea with the big pair of glasses without missing a square yard of it, resting my eyes by frequent calls on the VHF: nothing, only the lonely and hollow shriek of that interminable bloody gale which had stopped veering but had settled in the west and seemed to increase in violence.

After the fourth or fifth round of this Mackenzie came out of the chart-room asking if anything was wrong with the scanner of the navigational radar. It was mounted above the wheel-house and, when I took a look, it was stopped and mangled in appearance. I now knew what that serious-sounding noise had been. A large piece of steel had struck it and wrecked it.

'Radar's fucked, sir,' I reported, 'damaged in the explosion.'

It was Mackenzie's turn to say: 'Shit!'

He struggled forward and hauled himself up into the Captain's chair, which was lashed securely and seemed to sink into a brown study. I reported nothing to be seen, more to see if he was conscious than anything else.

He roused from an obvious stupor. 'Keep looking!' he snapped uncharacteristically.

'Aye, aye, sir.'

Out I went again and then I head Corrigan shout: 'Mr Childe! The VHF!'

I ran back into the wheel-house. Mackenzie's eyes were closed, his head dropped forward onto the breast of his duffle-coat, but Corrigan was wide-eyed.

'What is it?'

'I heard summat on the VHF!'

I picked-up the hand-set; '*if only*,' I found myself saying. '*If only.*'

'*Weather Guardian* to Number One boat, come in, over…'

Nothing…

'*Guardian* to Number One boat…'

I repeated the ritual several times but there was no response. 'You must've been mistaken, Corrigan,' I said.

'I heard summat,' he persisted. 'Definitely…'

And then the little miracle began. The intercom burst into life. 'Met. to Bridge.'

At first I thought they were ready for a balloon flight and I was ready to tell them to forget it, but then I realised that it was past 18.00 hours. We discovered later that the radio-sonde had been launched right on time, when the Old Man had the con and in spite of us being in the middle of an ocean rescue!

'Bridge to Met.'

'Met. here. Are you looking for the other boat?' It was Ted's voice.

'Yes,' I responded curtly.

'Well it's following us…'

I didn't wait for anything more, but dropped the intercom mike and left it dangling on its flex. I had quartered the sea assiduously; how could I possibly have missed…

At the after end of the port bridge wing I raised the binoculars. Even now I did not see it. The blind arcs behind various upstanding structures, narrow though they were, had deceived me. Besides, I had found hefting the big Barr & Stroud 7x50 glasses in the wind and with an arm badly bruised by the boat's tiller and further damaged by falling wreckage – the extent of which I did not know at this time of heightened tension – had not made my searching as sedulous as I had thought.

But then I saw her, coming up astern, small and insignificant, but with Pennington tall and dark in her stern and one mitigating fact that eased my conscience: I had been seeking an orange boat and the little cockleshell coming up astern as fast as her Thorneycroft diesel could drive her was dark, blackened, the paint stripped from her.

I went back into the wheel-house. 'We've got her!' I announced triumphantly.

My elation was short-lived, for Mackenzie was still slumped in the bridge-chair and, when I went through into the chart-room to tell the Old Man, Bill Wallis, the Second Steward, was packing his gear back in his bag. He shook his head.

I looked at poor old Duncan Gordon. He lay half on-half off the chart-room settee, fast asleep.

Bill said: 'I think he might be a bit concussed. We need to get him into his bunk…'

'You'll need a Neil-Robertson stretcher for that,' I said hurriedly. 'I've got to get the other boat back, can you handle him?'

Bill nodded.

I returned to the wheel-house and, by way of the intercom, called-out the boat-deck davit party. Fortunately it could now be augmented by my boat's crew. Leaning over the after end of the starboard bridge wing I could see No. 1 Boat coming up astern of us. Pennington was waving at us and I waved back. He must have seen me for he stopped his antics.

I held up both arms, palms towards him, meaning for him to stop where he was. For a moment I wasn't sure if he had either seen or understood me and then I noticed the bow-wave of the boat fall away and she turned up into the seas. I waited until I could see men on the boat-deck below me. When I saw the Bosun I shouted out: 'Bose!'

The Bosun looked up. 'Can you handle the pick-up, Bose?' I called down to him. 'The Old Man and the Mate' (meaning Mackenzie) 'are both barely conscious up here…'

The Stornowegian stalwart said nothing but raised his hand in acknowledgement. Ducking back into the wheel-house I went up to Mackenzie.

'We're ready to pick No. 1 Boat up, sir.'

Mackenzie grunted.

'Shall I carry on, sir?'

There was no response. I turned to Corrigan. 'You'll witness that I asked, Corrigan, won't you?'

'Aye, sir.'

'Right then…' I rang on Full-Ahead and, grabbing the intercom ordered the after deck cleared and the boat recovery party mustered in shelter on the boat-deck. I waited a moment or two as the old *Guardian* gathered up her skirts, drawing away from No. 1 Boat about three cables before ordering Corrigan to put the wheel over hard a-starboard. Round she came in that tight, sub-hunting turning circle, rolling as she did so with seas breaking on her port quarter with a violence that made her old hull shudder. Eventually she came all the way round – reversing her heading with the wind and sea astern. Then I steadied her with No. 1 Boat fine to starboard, driving down past her at a full 15 knots, leaving her a short distance to starboard before I threw the helm over to starboard again.

After all these years, I can flatter myself and say that Duncan Gordon could not have done it better himself (but perhaps it was beginner's luck!), and perhaps the old ship herself took a hand in recalling one of her missing chickens. But we came round again under full helm, our low stern swinging first to leeward and the whole ship rolling abominably to port – her heavier side now that No. 2 Boat was stowed in the port davits again. And still the ship turned, re-passing No. 1 Boat, but this time curving round 'up' her port side. White faces stared up at me, uncertain I supposed at what on earth I was doing, but I took no notice. I couldn't afford to. Still turning, the *Guardian*'s head passed through the wind and sea, her low stern slamming up to windward with more shocks and tremors felt throughout the ship and the whole of her hull laying down a most – to my eye – beautiful 'smooth' as I crash-stopped her with a double-ring of 'Full-Astern' on the telegraph.

Then, from the bridge, with two extended arms I frantically waved Pennington in under the davit falls. He needed no second bidding. With the Third Engineer crouching over the engine and the *Sunrise Victory*'s pathetic survivors squatting in her waist, Pennington completed his own triumph and ran No. 1 Boat under the starboard davit blocks.

Without giving it any attention at the time, I noticed he put away the after boat-axe before tackling the after block, but I did see blood on his right hand, visible even from the bridge. But my mind was wholly willing them all down there to accomplish the hooking-on and the hoisting without further ado. I need not have worried; Pennington and his bowman succeeded in the first and the Bosun and his men completed the second as I felt

– quite extraordinarily – my legs begin to shake uncontrollably, so-much-so that I could barely stand, and was sort of hanging over the after bridge rail, willing myself to get a grip.

*

Hanging there like a rag-doll I watched Pennington see his charges out of the boat and onto the boat-deck. He idly kicked aside pieces of the *Sunrise Victory* that seemed to him to be in their way. After the boat had been emptied of its passengers, as the Bosun supervised the davits hauling it up into the stowed position, I saw that the damage heat and fire had done to it. No wonder I had not been able to see the bloody thing!

I had mastered myself and was standing upright by the time Pennington reached the bridge to make his report. He stared about him, stuck his head in the chart-room, then looked at me as I leaned against the starboard wheel-house door which I had just shut behind me.

'Christ, it's like the last act of Hamlet up here, Jamie! And so it was you that had the con just now, picking me up?'

I shrugged, noticing but not really taking it in, that he was soaking wet, sea-water pooling round him on the deck. As for who had had the control of the ship, well, it was obvious wasn't it? I didn't want a big thing made of it. Pennington turned to Corrigan on the wheel but jerked his head towards me. 'It *was* him wasn't it, Corrigan?'

'Aye, sir, it were Mr Childe.'

'Mr Childe-with-an-*e*,' the dumbest, blindest fuckwit in the Western Ocean who couldn't see an elephant if it stood in the room next to him!' he bellowed at me, suddenly letting rip. 'I've followed you half the bloody way to Newfoundland, you damned numbskull, with a boat-load of hypothermic psychopaths off a fucking gun-running Panamanian tramp on Christmas fucking Eve of all fucking days of the fucking year…!'

'That's hardly…' I interjected, intending to say 'fair,' but Pennington had not finished with me, his diatribe rolling over my feeble protest.

'But Oh, God bless you Jamie!' he went on, 'God bless you, you are the best Christmas present a wandering albatross could have and looking round here I am not the only one who thinks so!'

I too stared round the wheel-house. There seemed little to justify Pennington's sudden change of tone. Mackenzie showed only marginal signs of life and little of sentient thought and, through the chart-room black-out curtain poor old Gordon had slumped onto the deck, Bill Wallis having left him some time earlier, either to attend to the new influx of survivors somewhere down below, or to fetch that stretcher. For a long and uncertain moment I thought Pennington had completely lost his marbles, which, had it been the case, would have rather left me as the last man standing.

But just as before, at an impasse, the ship pressed her needs upon me and, just as before, the engine-room telephone rang. I jumped towards it.

'Bridge, Third Officer speaking.'

'How long are you deck-ornaments going to hang around, eh? Ah've got two boilers cooking ma bollocks off doon here, dye want all this extra steam, cos if not Ah'll bank it fur a Christmas present…'

'Hang on, Chief.' I rang the telegraph to 'Full-Ahead,' waited a moment and then gave it the triple ring of 'Full Speed Away.' I took a look out of the wheel-house window and said, guessing wildly, 'Steer Oh-Four-Oh, Corrigan.'

'Oh- Four-Oh, sir,' replied Corrigan passing a few spokes through his hands.

Then the intercom. blared out, 'Met. to Bridge.' I responded and was informed, quite matter-of-factly, that the 18.00 hours balloon ascent had ended at a creditable 85,000 feet and 359 miles down wind. I recognised Ted's voice.

'Very good,' I said. 'And thanks for seeing the boat, I hadn't.'

'No problem, Jamie. D'you want me to come up and help you with any more of your duties?' he guyed me.

I considered the matter. 'You might have to Ted,' I responded, 'there are not many of us standing up here. It's been a bad day at Black Rock…'

I heard him chuckle and behind me Pennington said, 'I'm impressed young Jamie-with-an-*e*-Childe, most impressed…' I could see his eyes twinkling and I realised that I was bloody glad to have him back aboard, bloody glad he was not mad – or at least not mad enough not to know what to do, for he went on: 'Now, since we're heading roughly in the right direction, let's take stock…'

And with that we began to sort out the ship.

5

'Ye're back, Mr Pennington…'

'Safe and sound, Mr Mackenzie, thanks to young James here,' Pennington said as the First Officer stirred in the bridge chair and pulled himself together.

'You're bleeding,' I said to Pennington, indicating his right hand, which was covered in blood. 'And you're soaking wet!'

'It's nothing,' he replied, though I noticed he had begun to shiver.

Mackenzie groaned as he moved and, taking him by way of the outside ladders, rather than down through the internal vertical hatch, we got him down below to the wardroom where Chris Gilshaw and Bill Wallis had set up their casualty clearing station.

'I'll be up for the Old Man in a moment,' Bill said apologetically.

'Don't worry,' I replied. 'he's okay for a bit where he is.'

There were quite a few of the survivors, mostly from Pennington's boat, who required patching up, though none appeared to be seriously injured beyond cuts, scratches, some fairly lurid bruising and a great deal of shock. A plentiful supply of hot, sweet tea was on tap from the ward-room pantry and being dispensed by the Pantry-boy. Once dealt with, all except those obviously officers, judging by the variety of quasi-uniform clothing they were wearing, were sent to either the Petty-Officers' or the Ratings' messes, 'Except for that bastard there,' ordered Pennington.

We settled Mackenzie onto one of the ward-room settees and straightened up and regarded one of the sailors from the *Sunrise Victory*. 'He,' said Pennington contemptuously, looming over this wretch, 'came at me with a knife so, we're going to throw you into the brig, *amigo*.'

Several of the Met. Assistants were helping out with the first-aiding and other members of the crew were hovering about, so it was the work of a moment to rustle-up a couple of hard Glaswegians to escort the offending sailor forward. There was no 'brig,' of course, but there was a near empty, lockable dry-store at the forward end of one of the alleyways into which this fellow was promptly thrown. He offered little resistance, the piss and wind being blown out of him by his experience and the intimidating presence of our extempore 'policemen.'

'Thank you, gentlemen,' Pennington said cordially as he turned the key. 'We'll sort him out later.'

He turned to me. 'Get back on the bridge, Jamie. I'm going to change into some dry clothes…'

'You're shivering man, you'll get hypothermia…'

'Not after a brisk towelling down,' he insisted. 'Now get yourself topside. There's only Corrigan on the wheel. I'll be up there again in a jiffy.'

Back on the bridge I found Captain Gordon in better shape. He was sitting up on the chart-room settee, nursing his head, engaged in a shouted dialogue with Corrigan, still on the wheel and desperate for a piss.

'Where is the Officer-o'-the-Watch, Corrigan?' the Old Man was asking querulously.

'He's here, sir,' said a relieved Corrigan, who had perforce, been abandoned alone on the bridge. 'I need a piss, sir…' he said to me and I took the wheel and sent him down below, telling him to send up his relief, for his trick was long over and it was time to reimpose the ship's routine.

We got some hot-tea up on the bridge and, good as his word, Pennington soon arrived to take a look at the Old Man. 'It's not concussion,' he pronounced, at which Captain Gordon rallied, poo-pooing any 'sich nonsense'. Gradually he fully recovered his wits as Pennington outlined what had happened to him and his ship. He also rendered an abbreviated account of his own boat's experience, which I shall come to shortly, when I relate our later conversation on the subject. For the time being there were other priorities.

Ordering me to remain in charge on the bridge, Pennington took temporary command. He called the Chief Engineer, Chief Steward and the Department heads from Electronics, Radar and Met up to a pow-wow in the chart-room. With Captain Gordon sitting-in, Pennington told them that he thought Mackenzie had broken a couple of ribs and was likely to be out of action for twenty-four hours or so. Chris Gilshaw confirmed this, said he was terribly bruised and in a lot of pain. He should, Gilshaw thought, be got into his bunk as soon as possible.

To the question how many of other members of the crew were injured, it transpired that a few had acquired bangs and bruises, but that was mercifully all. Pennington stated that he and I could manage the bridge watches, but we'd need some assistance coping with the survivors. Turning to Chris Gilshaw he asked, 'How many of her officers escaped?'

'I think we've got two junior engineers, a Sparky and the Second and Third Mates. They're all pretty shocked and pretty useless at the moment.'

'They'll have to mess with us and bed down on the ward-room settees and deck.'

'We'll have to land them all as soon as possible too,' Pennington said, at which point Captain Gordon came out of his stupor with most of his wits functioning.

'We'll have to get permission to leave station, but being Christmas, this may take a day or two. I'll send a signal shortly asking to land them in Lough Foyle…'

I took little notice of the rest of the conversation. We got the watch-system back to a sort of normal. I would do until midnight, Pennington until 06.00, thereafter we'd work six hour watches, except that we never did after a few nights, for Captain Gordon took over the First Officer's four-to-eight. But I'm running ahead of myself, though I am not going to bore you further with these domestic details.

By midnight we were well on our way back to our proper station, rolling and scending, but speeding along. We effected the routine radio-sonde launch and Ted came up to the bridge for a few minutes, for an indulgently mutual catching-up of the ship's gossip. I complimented him on getting the balloon away at 18.00 amid the increasing drama of the ocean rescue.

'The Old Man told us we had five minutes,' he said in a tone that suggested a degree of indignation at the imposition. Being a relative new-comer to the life at sea, I don't think he realised quite what we had achieved in those conditions; he was fortunate Duncan Gordon had hove-to *that* long, given his other concerns with two boats, two officers and half the deck-hands away from the ship in a Force 9!

It didn't matter. Someone would explain before we got ashore so that he could go home and boast about the incident. Anyway, the barometer was rising at last and while Ted shared the end of my watch with me the wind chopped round, veering into the north-west quarter and within ten minutes the sky cleared and the temperature fell with the passing of the cold-front. Eventually, wishing me a happy Christmas, he went below.

Despite my own exhaustion I was reluctant to go below. I don't know why. After the extraordinary exertions of that awful day I was dog-tired, yet strangely energised, finding my second or third wind, so-to-speak. Perhaps it was the transformation of the weather, for the wind began to drop, the stars glittered and coruscated against the impenetrable black depth of the sky and the ship ran on under her two boilers, making an unprecedented (as far as I was concerned) sixteen knots.

I let Pennington sleep-in for an extra three-quarters-of-an-hour and even when he did appear, also wishing me a happy Christmas, I remained in the chart-room as he rubbed his wounded arm and drank his tea.

'D'you want me to have a look at that arm of yours?' I offered.

He shook his head. 'Bill Wallis cleaned it up pretty well and, for good measure, gave me a couple of anti-clap pills by way of anti-biotics!'

'Well,' I observed drily, 'you've the luck of a pox-doctor's clerk, so I guess you'll be alright.'

'You think I'm lucky?'

'I think that we're both fucking lucky!' I retorted. 'So's the ship and all who sail in her, for Heaven's sake!'

'Yes, we are… it's the magnetism thing, d'you see, Jamie? A preponderance of alignment… Here have one of these; Christmas present from Old Uncle Charles.'

He produced two Havana cigars, diverting me entirely – as, of course, he intended - from his remark about magnetism which, when I thought about it later, had been a few words to many.

I suppose adrenalin still ran through both of us, because I remained up there with him until just after 02.00, during which he told me what had occurred to No. 1 Boat.

After I had left him under the stern of the *Sunrise Victory*, he said, he had had trouble persuading the remaining members of the casualty's crew – 'about a dozen of them' - to jump into the sea. They were 'paralysed by fear until the fire came after them and was licking their arses like the Devil's tongues, by which time they'd left it damn nearly too late!'

He'd picked them all up, except two, who refused point-blank to leave. Meanwhile those already in the boat 'were panicking about the explosive cargo going bang. I had an altercation with one of them, that fellow we shut in the slammer, who came at me with a knife. Handling the boat and warding off the bastard allowed him to get in a slash at my arm,' here he held up his bandaged right arm by way of corroborative evidence, 'but my clothing saved me from too much damage and I got hold of the boat axe and told him in no uncertain terms I'd kill the cunt unless he sat down and shut up.'

I believed Pennington would have done just that too.

'Ironically,' he went on, 'this little melodrama saved us, because when the explosives detonated three things were in our favour. The first was that our proximity tucked up under the vessel's stern saved us from almost all of the blast; the second was that up on the poop either the blast or the blue funk, sent that last pair of reluctant sailors over the rail as though God Almighty had chucked them!' He paused. I liked the mixed metaphor: first the Devil then God, but I knew what he meant.

'And the third?' I prompted.

'Well, that was rather amazing…miraculous…though probably preordained,' which I thought an odd thing for him to say at the time, except that he had escaped death and needed to be cut some slack. 'I've seen it before,' he said almost reluctantly. I couldn't judge much from his face, of course, not properly in the distorting red night-light of the chart-room, but the tone of his voice suggested that it cost him some effort to recount this part of his narrative. At the time I didn't associate it with any crack-pot theories about magnetism and the uterine passage, particularly as he then gave it a quasi-academic gloss: 'And I've read about it too…'

All I took in was that his voice picked up as though the

vicariously acquired knowledge liberated him from some constraint.

'Anyway,' he went on, 'having been shielded from the blast our proximity to the seat of the explosion actually saved us. Most of the energy released went vertically then out and over our heads, falling back into the sea in a sort of rough circle of a radius of - oh, I don't know - two or three cables.'

'Probably about four,' I said. 'We got a load of it, as you saw, that's what buggered the navigational radar.'

'Well there you are then,' Pennington said. 'Thereafter, we picked up the two last guys and had to chase you half way to Newfie. St. John's.'

'I thought it was New York,' I said drolly.

'Oh well. I was exaggerating then, I'm being more truthful now,' he chuckled. 'For the purposes of historical veracity let's settle on Cape Farewell.' He paused. 'So there you have it: the complete and incontrovertible saga of No. 2 Boat…'

I didn't know about 'incontrovertible,' but a question occurred to me and I voiced it. 'How come you were soaking wet?' I asked, adding, 'and how come your boat was badly burnt so that *it was rendered bloody nearly inconspicuous to me*?'

Pennington was awkwardly silent for what seemed like several minutes before he lowered his voice and said, 'if I tell you, Jamie, I want your word that you'll keep quiet. I've told the boat's crew to keep their gobs shut and the Pandahooligans won't say anything after the barney in the boat. Okay?'

'Okay.'

'I don't know what was aboard that bloody ship, but apart from explosive material of some sort – and maybe her Second Mate can tell us later this morning, but as well as dynamite or tonite or whatever the hell it was, she had some flammable liquid, I guess in drums as deck cargo. It wasn't a lot or most of it went up in a bang with the rest, but some caught fire and ran down over the surface of the sea and I had to take the boat through it. It was a bit alarming at the time…'

I sensed a masterpiece of English understatement here, but it still did not explain everything.

'Was that to pick up the last two men?' I pressed.

'It was, yes.'

'And then?'

'And then what?'

'You didn't get as wet as you were from spray. You had to jump in and get them, didn't you?'

'Well… I suppose I did…'

'You *suppose* you did!' I snorted. 'For fuck's sake…'

'Keep your voice down,' he hissed at me, and I sensed the man at the wheel had his ears out on stalks.

'Sorry, Charles, but it is my turn to be impressed,' I countered in as conspiratorial tone as I could manage.

'It was nothing,' he said dismissively, stirring from his place on the chart-room settee.

I don't know whether it was my lack of sleep, the dynamic effects of adrenalin, or those of a sort of euphoric excitement after a day such as we had had, but I blurted out: 'It was more than that! I know you've a DSC and Bar!'

'Who…how did you know that?' he sounded genuine shocked and I felt almost shameful, for although not a capital offence, even prying into a book lying on one's bunk-shelf was a bit of a bloody cheek. Glad that he could not see my face flush under the red-lighting, I shrugged and said, 'Oh, I don't know, one of the lads, I think,' meaning one of the sailors.

'Not Archie McGrigor?'

'I can't remember,' I said hurriedly, 'but no I'm sure it wasn't him…'

A rather strained silence descended on us, then he stood up and said, 'well, perhaps it doesn't matter. You know now, but I don't go in for heroics, despite what the Old Man seems to think.' And I remembered Gordon's caveat to us during his briefing, and his earlier revelation that Pennington had been decorated for some unspecified act of wartime gallantry. 'Anyway,' Pennington stretched, 'thanks for the extra kip. One of us had better keep a watch and you look pooped-out, so finish that cigar and…'

'You sent me to your cabin,' I said almost before I had thought of doing so. I didn't want to mention the Old Man's comments. 'I saw you had a copy of *The Cruel Sea* by Monsarrat. It's one of my favourite books, and I took a look inside…'

'Oh, I see…the flyleaf with Nicholai's dedication. Huh! Why didn't you say so?'

'I think I thought you might have thought that I'd been prying.'

'Well you were. But I might have done the same in your place.' He paused. 'Yes, I do have a DSC and Bar. Long time ago… world's a different place now…rather forget about it all.' He drew heavily on the cigar, then ground it out in the adjacent ash-try. It was only half smoked and I thought it a waste. 'Anyway,' he said with a bitter little laugh, 'it did me precious little good… But you don't want to hear all that crap. It belongs to the past.'

I did very much want to hear all that crap, but I was being dismissed. Again I had that feeling that I should obey Pennington, call him 'sir' when I bade him good-night, but he swept out of the chart-room to take a look about us.

I took my cigar below; there was a hoolie in Chris Gilshaw's cabin and I accepted a scotch-and-water as we exchanged Christmas greetings, but ten minutes later my head fell forward and I apologised, abandoning the revels and turned-in.

*

Though I had slept unusually well, after less than four hours' kip I was totally knackered when I was called just before 06.00. Remembering that it was Christmas Day, I stuffed into the breast pocket of my battle-dress the letter that Sukie had sent me by way of the mail-drop and which I had been saving. There was a small package to accompany it, which I fondled lovingly before that went in my right-hand trouser pocket. I left the rather larger parcel and card that came quite obviously from my widowed mother as a treat for later. On the bridge Pennington handed over to me; we were back on station, back on one boiler and lying a-hull, the balloon launch having just taken place. The wind was still from the north-west, the sky was still clear and, annoyingly, I had to take a set of stellar observations. It was only after I had done this, by which time the ship was stirring into life, that I made myself a cup of tea and took Sukie's letter out of my pocket. As there was nothing in sight I retreated into the chart-room where the Eddystone radio was tuned in to a programme of Christmas carols.

And then the second explosion occurred, a rather personal one: eagerly opening Sukie's letter I found that she had sent me a 'Dear John…' I was being ditched, dumped, repudiated…

I remember crushing her pathetically short and dismissive letter and walking out onto the bridge-wing where I cast it overboard, remarking out-loud, 'What a charming fucking Christmas present!' looking up I had trouble focussing on the line of the horizon.

I ran through the usual gamut of foul language common to such occasions, wondering who the 'other fellow' was. Apparently he was all that I was not, and I felt petulantly certain he could not have handled a ship's boat in a Western Ocean gale, let alone a fourteen hundred ton ex-fucking frigate. I suddenly felt very tired and awfully alone, utterly fed-up and totally disenchanted. Then I remember the small package;

surely she hadn't…

But she had. I fished it out and opened the wrapping paper, snapping open the little box. There it nestled in some faux silk bedding, a diamond ring we had bought together in Hatton Garden a year earlier. 'Fuck!' I said, and it followed the letter overboard. 'Fuck!' I repeated, remembering that the salesman had said, with a mixture of coy solicitude, that he would buy the bloody thing back – at a small loss, of course – 'if things did not work out.'

Thankfully a much restored Captain Gordon came on the bridge to give me my breakfast relief. He was particularly complimentary about my conduct the previous day. I hope that I was at least civil to him, for I liked and respected him very much. Unfortunately Sukie had control of both my brain and my emotions and I was not master of myself.

By the time I got to the ward-room all of the other officers had broken their fast. Only the Yankee officers from the *Sunrise Victory* were at the table. They were affable and effusive in that casually charming way Americans are, expressing their personal 'gratitood' to me for my part in saving their lives. One of them pulled out his wallet and showed me a photo of 'His Girl back in Old Virginny' whom he would impress with a tale of the 'young Limey Mate,' who had preserved her 'Big Lover-Boy'. But when I quizzed them about their cargo and their voyage they clammed-up. Despite the fact that it had been an American voice that had told me about the consignment of whatever it had been, neither of the two deck-officers seemed to know much about the cargo, which had, they assured me, been 'the business of the Skipper and the Mate.'

I could have told them that I did not believe them, that I had served in cargo-liners and knew full-well that the Second and Third Mates knew what their ship's lading was. I suppose they thought we in the British Ocean Weather Service were para-naval, but I let it go. It was Christmas, after all and Big Lover-Boy was saved for His Girl, so with God in his Heaven all was right with the world.

Except that it bloody well wasn't.

As I prepared to return to the bridge for an extended morning watch I heard from somewhere down aft in the crew's accommodation, the sound of men singing Silent Night. I learned later that most of the *Sunrise Victory*'s Tex-Mex crew were Roman Catholics and they had asked if they could hold a service. A number of our people had joined them. Under any other circumstances I would have been moved by the occasion.

I had always thought that it was a tribute to the Christian religion that the joys of this mid-winter celebration of the birth of Christ could lift the spirits of every bunch of hard-nosed mariners I had ever sailed with – and this would be my seventh successive Christmas at sea. Men walked the bucking alleyways with a lighter tread, became more than cordial with each other and even smiled more than was customary. But I was in no mood for this sentimentality that Christmas. What the fuck was the point of singing *Silent Night* on Christmas morning?

Besides, there was a corpse lashed on the after-deck awaiting disposal; no-one seemed to have given this a second thought.

By 10.30 that forenoon I was thoroughly pissed-off. I spent more of that extra-long watch on the bridge wings than usual, which was somewhat unkind to Archie and Hamish, but I was saved at around eleven o'clock.

About ten minutes earlier we had rolled our way to leeward sufficiently far from *Oscar Sierra* to require us to get under way, so we were steaming slowly up-wind when there was what sounded like an odd flurry in the sea on our starboard beam. Curiously I peered over the rail; something was running alongside us, right alongside us, rubbing itself against the ship's shell-plating. Then, fifty yards out, leaping like dolphins in an

American tourist aquarium, two Orca rose out of the sea. There were three more further away, and one seemed to be 'sky-watching,' standing on its tail to observe us.

'Hamish!' I called to the Deck-boy.

'Fucking hell!' he breathed in awed wonder.

'Not a bad Christmas present,' I said, reliving McGrigor on the wheel for a few moments, so that he could have a look.

The pod remained with us for about twenty minutes, the nearest pair, a male and a female, gambolling with the agility of a much smaller cetacean, for these were big, mature killer whales. Sharply black and white they were a magnificent sight that – at least for a while – drove off my gloomy thoughts, so that I was in a reasonably congenial mood when, at 12.30 and after six and a half hours, I finally went down to the ward-room for a Christmas dinner that a replete Pennington declared to have been 'not half bad.'

The ward-room was still full. Those officers not relieving their colleagues remained at table, lingering over their brandies, itself a rare concession, and two half-empty bottles of claret invited the latecomers to catch-up. The turkey was good and had all the traditional trimmings and while not splendid - in an Ocean Weather Ship no meal was ever that – demonstrated that when the Chief Steward released sufficient goodies, the Cook could, in fact, cook. Even the Yanks seemed to approve, lashing in to the alcohol, used as they were to 'dry' ships.

Those of us with some experience of this knew that there would be a 'downer,' in the aftermath of a good dinner, some wine and other good cheer; that the days following would be bleak, until we wound ourselves up for the Bacchanalia of Hogmanay but that didn't matter that Christmas. Sukie aside, we had accomplished a major rescue less than twenty-four hours earlier and, quite apart from the religiosity or otherwise of the occasion, we had something very real to celebrate.

A group of us ended the day – and began Boxing Day - in the Chief Steward's cabin, enjoying a few gins. It was a stupid thing to do because, in consequence, my personal downer began on Boxing Day. At 05.45. I dragged myself out of my bunk and made my way up to the bridge. I won't bore you with the tedious miseries of unrequited love at the age of twenty-two combined with a mild hang-over but accompanied by a rising sea. Actually, although the sea was rough it was a fine day with bright, sunny patches, a big swell and a bracing breeze during which we had about fifty pilot whales snorting malodourously round the ship. We carried out a deep-sea sounding with our Nansen bottles, after which a number of us, including several of the crew of the *Sunrise Victory*, mustered on the after deck for the burial of the man who had died, now identified as Angelo Gonzales.

It was a sad little affair, the one blemish upon our achievement, but it was accomplished with all that quiet dignity that a rough group of seamen could confer on the occasion. The Old Man conducted the brief service and I recall he intoned: 'Man that is born o' woman, hath but a short time tae live, he goes up like fore-topmast staysail and comes doon like a flying jib.'

That evening we had the Petty Officers and ratings into the wardroom for Christmas drinks. Iain Mackenzie got out of his bunk for this, shoving aside our protests that he should take it easy and dismissing our concerns.

'Ye ken fu' well that if Ah ha' broken ma ribs there's nothin' tae be done, sa Ah'll be on watch this afternoon at sixteen hunder hoors. Ah canna ha' ye youngsters takin' ower the bluidy ship altogether…'

I think that he rather resented the fact that Pennington and I had somehow 'robbed' him of the glory of completing the task that he had been so instrumental in starting. Moreover, this had something to do with Pennington's age and his previous, mysterious 'experience'. What the Old Man thought of it all, I don't know, but he moved easily among our 'guests,' laughing and joking, much admired – they told me later – by our other guests, the American officers from the *Sunrise Victory*.

Pennington had released his prisoner from the slammer on condition that the man apologised and promised 'on the Holy Virgin' that he would behave himself. Thereafter the fellow behaved himself.

'Heat of the moment,' Pennington said to me when he relieved me that night. 'Anyway, before I gave him his liberty, I got it out of him that the *Sunrise* was bound for Hodeidah and she was carrying arms among an otherwise legitimate cargo of "lumber" and chemicals… an odd mixed cargo for a tramp, don't you think?'

'I suppose so,' I responded. 'The explosives were for who? The Yemeni rebels?'

'Yes. And there were arms, or at least ammunition, because – and no-one else in the boat seemed to notice this – there were some rather nasty things shooting out of the water at one point. The rest I presume to have been heavily over-stowed by the timber so that no-inquisitive inspector could find them without first discharging the ship.'

'That would explain why they took so long to ignite, the timber would burn slowly – hence their decision that they should cancel their original Mayday…'

'Exactly so. Nor would they want to be discovered to be carrying a war contraband by any salvor – anyway, that will all be forgotten since the whole lot lies on the abyssal plain, or stuck in some mountain pass of the mid-Atlantic ridge.'

'Well,' I added, 'there's an awful lot of that sort of thing littered about the sea-bed in these latitudes.' I was thinking about my poor father.

'*You're* telling *me*?' Pennington responded with a curious twisting of emphasis that recalled me to the fact that he had seen a good deal of it on its way to the ocean's bottom during the Battle of the Atlantic.

'Sorry, I wasn't really telling granny how to suck eggs,' I said ruefully. I forbore telling him about my father.

'No, I know you weren't. Anyway, time for you to get some shut-eye.'

'Yeah.' I didn't move until he nudged me.

'Go on. Fuck off. It's time for your beauty-sleep.

6

The following morning we received orders to proceed to Lough Foyle and discharge the survivors of the *Sunrise Victory*. This was essential; although we had some basic emergency rations, the *Guardian* was only victualled for a limited number of people and for a specific number of weeks. We continued operating as Ocean Station INDIA as we worked our way diagonally across the grid, changing our radio-beacon identification letters until the edge of the lattice. Thereafter we steamed at full speed, both boilers roaring away and scending along in a wild following sea. We cut inside Inistrahull Island at sunset the following evening, I think it must have been, in a spectacular sea, streaked with white and gold as we ran over the shallows and entered Lough Foyle. We eventually got all the *Sunrise Victory*'s survivors ashore by way of the pilot cutter and another launch which brought us out supplementary stores from Moville. By midnight we were on our way back to station, banging our way to windward again.

Although we deck-officers had had to submit written reports about our parts in the rescue from which Captain Gordon had compiled his full *Report of Proceedings* (which had been landed at Moville), we doubted that we would ever hear anything more about the incident. Only one life had been lost, and that by virtue of an ill-advised and precipitate jump, so it was extremely unlikely that the Panamanian authorities would launch an enquiry. The Panamanian Registry was, in any case, operated by a private agency out of an office in New York whose principal duty was farming the dues paid for the privilege of wearing their flag-of-convenience and, after mulcting it of its commission, passing the residue to the Panamanian government. Such a neat business scam allowed dodgy cargoes to be carried about the seven seas, simultaneously reducing running costs – including those of ship surveys, crew wages and so forth. It may have changed today, but that was not the case back then. Indeed, the chief purpose of Gordon's *Report* was to cover the total destruction of our bridge radar, some other dents and bent fittings injured by sundry parts of the disintegrating *Sunrise Victory*, and the fire-damage to No. 1 Boat – though most of this last was superficial and could be dealt with in Greenock.

Reaching the outer graticules of the grid we resumed out duties as Ocean Station INDIA and in due course found ourselves back in grid square *Oscar Sierra*. And there we sat, the days passed as we carried out our various duties, Hogmanay came and went and I began to have distinctly mixed feelings about the end of the voyage. The primary reason I had joined the Ocean Weather Service had evaporated and it must have been obvious that I had changed, for twice when I relieved him for his evening meal relief – another of my duties - Iain Mackenzie asked me if I 'was alright'.

Late one night the Old Man came on the bridge to sign his night orders and tackled me with the same question. Of course I batted all such enquiries aside and made efforts to cast off these blues, but the lack of proper sleep and the low-level unpleasantness of our environment made such psychological adjustments difficult.

In the end it was Pennington who nailed me. It was our last night on the central grid. We would set off for the edge the following morning to rendezvous with *Weather Follower* and hand over to her before high-tailing it to Greenock. I had long since decided to hand in my resignation at the end of the present voyage, so perhaps such a moment of near consummation, my final one *Oscar Sierra* – On Station.

As was usual my hand-over was actually a few minutes after the midnight balloon launch. Moreover, I tarried, enjoying a cup of tea with Pennington, for – systemically tired though I was – I had no great desire for my pit, despite the fact that the ship was unusually comfortable, relatively speaking anyway. The wind was a gentle Force 6 from the north-west, the sky was clear, though a hefty cross-swell from the west threw us about a bit. We could hear the intercom traffic between Radar and Met. as the radio-sonde rose and drifted away to leeward, but we lay a-hull and, with nothing in sight, the two of us were sipping our tea in the chart-room.

'Time for your beauty sleep, Jamie,' Pennington said, trying to ease me off the bridge.

'I haven't finished my tea.'

'What's the matter? Aren't you eager to get home, is that it?' He asked with extraordinary prescience, eyeing me as I shrugged. 'Oh, I'm sorry. She's given you the heave-ho, hasn't she.' It wasn't a question.

'How d'you know?'

He chuckled. 'You've had it written all over your face since Christmas.'

'Have I?' I asked genuinely astonished.

'Well that's a figure of speech, of course, but to those of us sensitive enough to divine these things from emanating magnetic fields, your unhappiness has been…what shall I say? Palpable?'

'Really?' I was incredulous.

'Yup. Really.' He went to the chart-table and, opening one of the lower drawers, pulled out a chart, unfolding it and spreading it out on the chart-table. 'You see,' he said, smoothing it out in such a way that I felt compelled to stand next to him and stare down at the large sheet of paper. It was an American chart, a small scale map of the North Atlantic Ocean, covered by wavy lines. I recognised it immediately as our isogonic chart for the current epoch from which we took off the surface variation of the earth's magnetic field when calculating our compass error. Although we used a Sperry gyro-compass, we were obliged to carry an old-fashioned magnetic compass by way of back-up, and by taking regular Azimuths or the occasional Amplitude, applying the earth's variation, we could arrive at the deviation, or the effect of the ship herself on the accuracy of the magnetic compass. This was all a bit arcane, almost a tradition borne out of ancient necessity but, like some recondite religious rite, only a brave man would revoke the custom and gyro failures, though rare, were not unknown.

Anyway, Pennington was running his index finger over the isogons – the lines of equal magnetic variation – that ran through our rough position, babbling about the personal tribulations that occurred to individuals whose personal molecular magnetism was at distinct odds with the terrestrial field where we were: *Oscar Sierra* on Ocean Station INDIA.

'I am in an anomalous state here,' he confided, 'which was why I was apprehensive when the Old Man said I was to take one of the boats away – not for myself, you understand, for I have little regard for my own safety these days, but for the fact that being anomalous compromised my chances of success. Now you may be similarly compromised…'

'Hang on,' I interrupted. 'Are you suggesting the being dumped by my fiancée is somehow related to where we are?'

'Well yes, and where she was and who she was with when she made the decision to write you the Dear John letter.'

'Okay…' I said cautiously, trying to make sense of this odd

concept, 'but *if* I am, as you say and like you, in an anomalous state here,' and I leaned over and rather forcibly stabbed my own forefinger somewhere near where we were lying, 'then how come I too managed to pull-off my share of the rescue in No. 2 Boat?'

With the ship rolling and the two of us braced against the edge of the chart-table I remember us sort of twisting inwards and staring, the one at the other. I think I had a mixed expression of disbelief, truculence and probably a good touch of blatant ridicule on my tired mug. He, on the other hand, seemed – and don't forget his beard – to be regarding me as thick; that I had proved incapable of seeing the point, but with a twinkle of triumph in his own eyes, which gave me to understand he knew the answer to my heretical question.

'You don't understand, do you?'

'No, I bloody well don't.'

'Okay, first tell me, on your way in the boat towards the casualty, what were you thinking…in a word or two?'

'Well, how I was going to cope, whether I was going to be able to manage…all perfectly normal things to think about.'

'Of course. But be honest, you were apprehensive, weren't you?'

'I didn't have time to be scared, if that's what you're implying.'

'I'm not implying anything. But your mind-set was one of apprehension, eh?'

'Well, yes, wasn't yours?'

'Yes, of course.'

'Well then…'

'But once we got close to the *Sunrise*, all that disappeared, didn't it?'

'We had a job to do,' I said reasonably, 'wc focussed…at least that's what I did. I didn't go in for any heroics like you….'

'Because there was no need for them in your case,' Pennington went on soothingly, ignoring my insinuation, 'though you have no idea what you might have done if there *had* been. Anyway, let's leave me out of this. You admit, from anxiety you turned positive and got on with the job in hand; yes?'

'Yes.'

'And you attribute that to what?'

I shrugged. 'As I said focus, training, duty. Those guys needed rescuing… I don't understand what you're driving at.' I was growing truculent. I suddenly decided that I did need my bed; and soon.

'What I am driving at, Jamie, is that is all true – the brotherhood of the sea, mariners in distress and all that crap – but it wasn't just your training: who ever actually taught you to do what you did? Or your sense of duty by itself? No, no; it was having your magnetically anomalous self *changed* in that moment of extreme crisis because, let's be fair, it *was* quite an achievement.'

I was growing cross and frustrated. 'I just did my job,' I said shortly.

'Yes, yes, you did and you did it admirably,' Pennington countered with a patience that surprised me in its coaxing, 'and nothing, *nothing* diminishes *you* by what happened to you physically…'

I'd had enough. 'Oh for Chrissakes,' I said, turning back to the isogonic chart. 'Are you telling me that there I was, at one moment physically at odds with the earth's magnetic field and then my personal molecular magnetic structure was altered?'

'Yup!' Pennington said with a sort of triumphant snapping. 'That's *exactly* what I'm telling you. And you were right out of kilter on Christmas morning when you got your Dear John…'

'Well I suppose I brought that on myself then!' I said

indignantly.

'In a manner of speaking, though not directly, but your lack of congruence meant that it affected you badly…'

'Well of course it affected me badly!'

'But think about that evening we saw the aurora. You were transfixed that night, as was I.'

'But we were right here! On Station! In the same bloody place. So how..?'

'Because for that night this,' and it was his turn to stab the isogonic chart in mid-Atlantic, 'was all transformed by the effect of the aurora!'

'Are you sure about that? Or was it an augmentation, or just a visual manifestation of its presence? Surely…'

Pennington airily waved my equivocations aside as being of no consequence. 'Of course I'm sure, but with regard to the rescue itself, which is where the absolute proof of my hypothesis lies, consider the question of what provided the imposed and anomalous magnetic field that changed you, so that you acted positively.' He paused and stared at me. 'You still don't see it, do you?'

I was tired, and by now irritable, flustered and mentally mixed-up. My obvious misery was to do with a young woman dumping me, not the earth's magnetic field. I didn't mind Pennington having his loony notions; indeed he was entitled to them. In other circumstances I might have found them mildly interesting or amusing. Heaven knows, I had met enough religious and political theorists *and* practitioners during my six years at sea. Some I respected more than others, but I was beginning to dislike Pennington's debunking of my only claim to heroism. It was okay for him to pontificate, what with his DCS and Bar…

It was all very unworthy stuff on my part, and I would be ashamed of it later, but just then I was overdue for my bunk and had had enough.

'No!' I snapped, 'I don't see it…'

'The ship, Jamie, the ship! The *Sunrise Victory* herself! A great big chunk of steel with her own magnetic field, strong enough to realign both you and me… *She* was the magnetic anomaly that affected our much smaller, weaker human alignments.' He looked at me, his eyes glowing triumphantly, as he folded the isogonic chart and put it away.

There was a pause, and then I asked: 'you absolutely believe that, don't you?'

'Absolutely. I do not pretend to fully *understand* it, and I know I am laughed at for it, but – and here I say this to one of the very few people to whom I have ever spoken in depth about it, and that because here was a palpable truth with the *Sunrise* playing her benighted part – I have found it explains a good deal in my own life. We've reduced belief systems to stupid formulaic crap, or nutty psycho-babble, but the magnetic doctrine of the uterine passage, I believe, offers us a means of us disposing of such inchoate notions of having good or bad luck, of making one's own luck, or of surviving, or the reverse when *in extremis*.'

I think I may have smirked, even sniggered a tad at poor Pennington's use of the portentous phrase 'the magnetic doctrine of the uterine passage,' but I held my tongue and if he noticed he made nothing of it, for he was deadly serious.

'As I said, you are one of the few people I have been frank with and I would not have been so with you, had you not discovered that I was given a couple of decorations during the war. They did me no good; I am an ordinary chap; like you I lost the love of my life, except that it nearly destroyed me as it had destroyed my career and sent me out into the post-war world an albatross, to wander the oceans. Unlike me you'll find another someone and I wish you well.' H paused a moment then added: 'What I will say is don't go grovelling when you get ashore...'

I seized this slight curve the conversation had taken back to a normality. 'No, I won't be doing that. She sent the ring back in the mail drop. It's somewhere on Ocean Station INDIA.'

'Quite right too,' Pennington said. 'Now you'd better get some kip.'

*

The following midnight we were on the homeward run, relieved of our station by the *Weather Follower* shortly beforehand. I remember being eager to get home now. I had used the last hours on Ocean Station INDIA to ruminate on my fate, quite unaware then of anything in the way of advice that Pennington might have conveyed, either directly or subliminally. At the conclusion of my deliberations I had recalibrated my forthcoming expectations. There would be no grovelling, only a passing over, and I would fashion a different future to the one I had planned.

When he arrived to relieve me, Pennington sat as usual on the chart-room settee even though we had a ship in sight away to starboard. 'He's well away to the westwards,' Pennington said, drawing a rather battered looking brown envelope from the inside breast pocket of his battledress. Taking out a yellowing piece of white paper, he held it out to me without comment.

I took it and unfolded it. It was a medical certificate issued at Netley Hospital in Hampshire and it declared the named Lieutenant-Commander C. P. R. Pennington was now of sound mind.

'I know you think I am mad, James Childe-with-an-*e*,' he said with a smile that I could only perceive by the distortion of his beard, for his eyes seemed wistfully sad, 'but I at least have documentary proof to the contrary.'

*

We berthed in Great Harbour, Greenock, around noon a few days later and that evening, Ted Wilkins and I loaded our gear into the back of my old MG which I had collected from the garage that afternoon. I had said my farewells. Captain Gordon was good enough to write me a fulsome testimonial because, as he said, 'ye'll get nary a guid word frae that old buzzard Brownhall fur bailing oot o' the Sairvice quite sae soon.'

I had said goodbye to Iain Mackenzie in the ward-room where, just as on the day when I joined the *Weather Guardian*, he was chatting to Dougal Henty, waiting for Henty's wife to pick them both up. As for Pennington, he came down the gangway carrying my sextant box and tucked it into the car for me.

'Are you not putting the roof up?' Pennington asked quietly.

'Not unless it rains, and we didn't forecast any did we,' I remarked laughing.

'And I thought I had to convince you that it was me who was sane,' he said. It was the last remark I heard him make as Ted Wilkins and I clambered in and I fired-up the engine.

Turning back I waved at Pennington, now standing at the bottom of the gangway. He seemed a lonely figure and – quite unbidden – my heart went out to him. Then I let off the racing hand-brake, gunned the engine, let in the clutch and headed south.

*

That evening of departure I turned a page in my life; two pages actually, one personal the other professional. I neither saw nor heard of any one of my ship-mates from the *Weather Guardian* again. The British Ocean Weather Service was wound-up in the 1980s, when their work was taken over by increasingly sophisticated satellites. The remaining two British weather ships were scrapped; neither of them was the *Weather Guardian*, she had long gone to the breakers at Burntisland.

That was the last of it all, I thought, until, idly searching about on the internet one grim, grey, wet and windy afternoon many years later, with the glass dropping and the herring gulls screeching over my garden on the Suffolk coast, I happened across an entry in Wikipedia which seemed to have been lifted largely from an edition ofm *The Courier* of 1969.

It was the obituary of Lieutenant Commander Charles Penhallo Robert Pennington DSC and Bar, Royal Navy. It informed me 'this distinguished and controversial naval officer' had been 'found dead in his small cottage in Laugharne, near Carmarthen, on 23rd April 1969.'

It went on to say that:

'Pennington, born in 1910, only son to the Rev. T.H.P Pennington and his wife Mary (née Penhallo) of St Iltydd's, Pembrokeshire, had joined the Royal Navy by way of Osborne and Dartmouth. Whilst serving in the then Atlantic Fleet as a junior officer he had attracted the disapprobation of Their Lordships of the Admiralty when, in 1931 during the Great Depression, he favoured the cause of the Invergordon mutineers. The mutiny had been precipitated by a swingeing pay-cut chiefly affecting the petty-officers and ratings. Many married men were reduced to indigence and abject poverty. The young Pennington, expressing a sense of deep outrage, boldly claimed in an open letter to *The Courier* that the state had no right to deny a living wage to men prepared to risk their lives in the active service of their country. After an acrimonious legal process that attracted little notice at the time amid the events surrounding the mutiny, he was dismissed, joining the mercantile marine, where he obtained a Certificate of Competence as Master Mariner.

'When the country's call came in 1939, he resigned his post with the Blue Funnel Line of Liverpool, and volunteered as a naval rating, soon attracting the notice of others, being made a

Commissions and Warrants candidate (a man with officer potential). After a spell of training, Pennington was commissioned a sub-lieutenant in the summer of 1940. Thereafter, his rise was rapid; appointed to corvettes under the command of Flag-Officer Western Approaches, his mercantile training made him a natural navigating officer with the rank of lieutenant. By 1942 he was first lieutenant of HMS *Hawkbit* and by the time the Battle of the Atlantic reached its climax in the spring of the following year Pennington had command of a new frigate, HMS *Loch Shin*.

He took part in the escort of several convoys to North Russia, during which he located and single-handedly sank a U-boat before any of the other escorts could come to his assistance, for which he was awarded his first Distinguished Service Cross. He also made a name for himself for his attention to the rescue of survivors of torpedoed merchantmen, on one occasion defiantly disobeying the signalled order of the rear-admiral commanding the ocean escort who denied him the requested permission to leave the convoy's protective screen for this purpose. His disobedience saved the lives of twenty-eight men. He narrowly escaped a court-martial for this action, which won wide support from several sources in the aftermath of the disaster of Convoy PQ17, receiving enthusiastic support from Lord Southmoore's highly influential newspaper *The Courier* which was campaigning on behalf of merchant seamen. Nevertheless, in the eyes of the Admiralty, from this time on, he was a marked man.

'Others thought differently; his talents were too good to waste and in 1944, although unpromoted, Pennington was in 'temporary' command of a Support Group of two frigates and three corvettes working in the North Atlantic, Pennington located a second U-boat, vectoring in the members of his Group to depth-charge their target, forcing her to the surface.

Unfortunately the U-boat sank before she could be salvaged, but the relentless attack lasting over six hours earned Pennington a Bar to his DSC.

'In 1942 he had married Isabelle, only daughter of Mr and Mrs Clive Woolmore of Cheshire. The couple settled in Liverpool where Pennington was based. Mrs Pennington became a popular figure in naval circles, but was sadly killed in the spring of 1944 by a V1 doodle-bug shortly after the couple moved to London following her husband's transfer to the Channel prior to the D-Day invasion.

'After the war Lt-Cdr Pennington was retired from the navy by Admiralty order. He petitioned against this, maintaining he had vindicated his earlier conduct and that his act of disobedience in the Barents Sea had not merited a court-martial. In this he over-played his hand. His application to be reinstated was turned down, as were a series of others which he pursued with the same doggedness he had worn down Doenitz's U-boats.

When he made a public appeal by a demonstration at Epson races he was arrested for disorderly conduct and, in a perversion of British justice, brought under Admiralty jurisdiction and formally cashiered as an alcoholic. There was little actual evidence for this, except that he was undoubtedly drunk on the occasion of his public demonstration at Epsom where, wearing his naval uniform, he sought to attract the notice of King George VI.

'Pennington was sent to the inter-services hospital at Netley near Southampton where he was held for 'treatment' for several years, being released in the summer of 1952. He was a friend of the popular novelist and pre-war journalist Nicholas Monsarrat, who encouraged him to write, but without much success. He was involved in the making of several war films before returning to his first love, the sea. After a spell yacht-crewing in the West Indies, Pennington became an officer in various tramp-ships until, around 1959, he gained a command with the Shun Feng Shipping Company of Hong Kong. Whilst in Hong Kong, about 1964, he became ill, and, following treatment back in Britain, is believed to have lived quietly in South Wales until his death from a cardiac arrest on 23 April.'

And that was it. No mention of his time in the Ocean Weather Service, so no clues as to who might have posted that death notice, except that it was someone who had no in-depth knowledge of the entirety of Pennington's life. Nor, I suspected with some conviction, had ever heard of the Ocean Weather Service, but who clearly wished full honours to be given to this extraordinary man.

But – to my shame in the pride of my youth - this was the fellow who I had mildly resented being promoted over my head as Acting Second Officer of the OWS *Weather Guardian*!

How bravely he had born his humiliation.

Perhaps too, this little auto-biographical account can put the record straight, should anyone be interested in either Pennington or the Ocean Weather Service, in which he ended his sea career.

Later still I discovered that he had been cremated according to his wishes, and his ashes had been scattered off Lundy Island from the Swansea-based Trinity House lighthouse-tender *Alert*. I wondered if, by his cremating, he had wanted to destroy the magnetic entity that he believed himself to be? Surely that was the only way he could find rest, widely dispersed by the fierce tides of the Bristol Channel. He could not have been buried, for to lay him in the cold Welsh earth contrary to the favour of the isogons would have almost certainly consigned him in to a private Purgatory. But if anything is ever found in his theory, it will presumably mean we are all magnetically charged and, being so prolific, cannot therefore be regarded as anomalies.

However, this is quibbling beyond my competence to comment on the details of Pennington's thinking. What I can say is that, not so long ago, about thirty sperm whales were washed up on both sides of the North Sea. Scientific consensus was that they had been misled by distortions to the terrestrial magnetic field upon which the sensory perceptions of their internal navigating systems relied. These distortions and their consequent disturbances to the whales was thought to have been caused by exceptional auroral activity.

Whatever the bigger picture, I hold to my own belief that, like the wreck of a steel ship on the sea-bed, Charles Pennington himself undoubtedly was a magnetic anomaly. Moreover, I think he thought little of his DSC and Bar; as far as he was concerned, he had just done his job. After all, it had been Monsarrat who had inscribed it in his book, not Pennington himself. I think that he believed that he had a talent for divining other magnetic anomalies: just as was the case with the *Sunrise Victory*, what more of such a thing was there than a U-boat? Remember, he had said to me with some emphasis that he was just 'an ordinary fellow,' or words to that effect.

Looking back now, after more than half a century has passed, I am proud to have known him. He was one of once *Great* Britain's long forgotten seamen who await the clear call of the last trump, when the sea shall give up its dead.

Printed in Great Britain
by Amazon

61825654R00090